# This Side of Water
## Stories

Maureen Pilkington

Regal House Publishing

Published by
Regal House Publishing, LLC
Raleigh, NC 27612
All rights reserved

ISBN -13 (paperback): 9781947548749
ISBN -13 (epub): 9781947548756
ISBN -13 (mobi): 9781947548763
Library of Congress Control Number: 2019930301

Interior and cover design by Lafayette & Greene
lafayetteandgreene.com
Cover image "Reflections" © by Erin Gregory
Author photograph by JoAnn Cancro Photography

Regal House Publishing, LLC
https://regalhousepublishing.com

Grateful acknowledgment is made to the following magazines, where these stories first appeared, some in slightly different form.

*Confrontation:* "Float"; *ThePedestalMagazine.com:* "Blue Tip Shore Club, New Year's Eve 1969"; *Puerto del Sol:* "Turquoise Water Behind Him"; *The SN Review:* "In The Beach Chair"; *The Antioch Review:* "Toward the Norwegian Sea"; *Marco Polo Quarterly:* "Sounds Skimming Over The Atlantic"; *SECRETS: The 2012 MSR Short Fiction Anthology:* "Not That Kind Of View"; *Confrontation:* "Dreaming Over The Monongahela, August 1911"; *Ploughshares:* "Nudes In A Green Pond"; *Red Rock Review:* "Crowded Pond"; *The Blotter:* "Must Be Near The Hudson"; *Orchid Literary Review:* "Two Pigs And A Circle of Palm Trees"; *Santa Barbara Review:* "The Water In Alexander Eyes"; *TheStoneTableReview.com:* "Holy Water"; *The Patapsco Review:* "Past The Club House"; and Miranda.com: "Effects Of The Waterfront."

For Mark Rossi

The sea pronounces something, over and over,
in a hoarse whisper: I cannot quite make it out.

— Annie Dillard

# Contents

# PHOSPHORESCENCE

# FLOAT

I swam out to the float alone, the one that was anchored farthest from the beach, and lay down between the seagull stuff that had dried in so many spots. From there I could see the beach club members at a beautiful distance. I could see Mr. Fieldings' orange fish waving above his cabana, and him, sitting in front of his domain, doing accounting on a bridge table in his bright orange bathing suit, the little kind that stretched like balloon fabric over his privates. He used rocks, as smooth and oval as eggs laid from large birds, to weigh down stacks of bills and orders from his liquor store. His wife still wore bikinis and gold loop earrings, because they had no children.

Mrs. Fieldings was the head buyer for Bergdorf Goodman over in Scarsdale and had me working there on Saturdays, modeling pre-teen dresses. She just pulled me off the diving board line-up one day and gave me this job that paid in clothes. Luckily, my friends never recognized me in a dress without my nose clip and hair as bone dry as the sand.

The Fieldings were landmarks to my left from my vantage point out on the float—the lifeguard, my center marker on his giant wooden high chair, and the snack bar at the other end, pumping up smoke signals all day long.

That Labor Day Weekend was no different from others I remembered, with the sky bluer and the view sharper like a true fall day; and every member was eating up their summer quota.

3

I turned away from the club and faced the open Long Island Sound. I put my ear on the hot, salty surface and heard the water lapping against the underside of the float. It reminded me of the sounds I'd heard the night before coming from the orange cabana.

Fort Slocum stood on a deserted island off to the right about two thousand yards from me. The fort didn't function anymore, but it stood tall like my father with hands on his hips and a take-no-prisoners attitude. I had heard that the island was infested with rats.

I heard a sloppy breaststroke coming at me and saw Mary Beth zig-zagging her way out to the float. Every few feet, she stopped and floated on her back for a minute to build up strength so she could make it the rest of the way. I think it was the french fries and dogs that slowed her down. Some of the kids called her *Miss Snack Bar '72*.

"What are you doing out here?" she panted, hanging on to the side, her hair stuck to her cheeks. Her eyes were always scanning the surface for a water rat that might have made its way across the sound for a visit.

"M.B. Can't you see I'm busy?"

"No."

Now she had one leg up, her foot in the white-crusted seagull droppings, but this kind of thing never fazed her.

"Come on, Nan, help me up."

"All right." I pulled her by two hands, and she slapped down hard on her ribs. "Come up to my office."

"What are you doing out here all by yourself?"

"Thinking."

"About what?"

"The situation."

Mary Beth was still breathing hard. Now there was white crust on her elbows.

"I want to go back," I said, eyeing the whereabouts of my parents. I could see that Mary Beth was too winded to go now and decided to wait.

"When are we going to do it?" she asked.

"Tonight is the last night of the summer."

I looked for Mom in her circle of chairs. All I had to do to find her was to look at which direction Mr. Fieldings was facing. He was in a sit-up chair, with Chivas Regal crates piled upside down in the shape of a side table. When you walked by their living room on the beach, you could hear the sound of ice scooping and falling into real highball glasses. He was getting up now, his skin oiled and evenly grilled to perfection.

I wondered what he saw in Mom when he had a wife like Mrs. Fieldings. Mrs. Fieldings always seemed to be waiting for the punch line, ready to burst out, and something was always swinging from her—a tiny gold chain-belt on her waist, the strings on her bathing suit that unraveled and fell to her golden sides, those earrings. Her entire orange bikini was made of triangles with a bow tied on each hip. Mom's was practically a skirt. But more than all of that, Mrs. Fieldings was really nice to me. I worked with her. I knew her. After my hours were done, she would take me to the pink-striped restaurant in Bergdorf's, which looked just like an ice cream parlor, and buy me the Kitchen Sink.

Mary Beth was staring at me, her cheeks on the verge of purple. "You sure it was them in there last night? Maybe it was Cheryl and Joe or someone from their group. They're always sneaking into the cabanas at night." Mary Beth was trying to make me feel better.

"No, I doubt it. They're going away to college, and they'll be able to do it anytime they want." I dove in and swam back to shore freestyle. When I got there, I turned around and saw Mary Beth was still halfway out, floating on her back.

I walked past the new tennis court, which was now crowded with women's doubles, their volleys hanging in the air too long. I found Dad behind the snack bar, in the horseshoe pit with the rest of the guys. My heart went out to him, knowing what I knew. He looked so content with a beer in his hand, the tattoo on his arm of an old ship bobbing and weaving over his muscle. He was almost as tan as Mr. Fieldings.

"Hey—sweetheart!" He waved for me to come over. When I got there he said to the guys, "Look at the arm on this kid."

He handed me the horseshoe. "OK, I'll give you a little leeway. Stand over there."

"Still tough," one of the men said.

I looked at my audience before I walked up to my spot. Mr. Patella had burgers stuffed in the sides of his mouth, doing a Marlon Brando. All the men had bloated stomachs, their belly buttons pulled like the knot in a balloon—except for Dad's, still tight as a drum. He liked to say his muscle tone came from laying sheet rock, not lying in the sun. Sometimes I saw Cheryl, the best-looking teenager who hung out at the lifeguard shack, checking him out.

"Shoot," Dad yelled. His streaked hair was glistening and the comb marks made deep rows as if a miniature plow machine worked the land of his head.

I stood on my marker and gave my best shot. I heard an immediate *clink*. A hit. This meant that Dad would give me a swig of beer. I walked to the keg area, confident. The men cheered and when I turned to catch Dad's eye he was observing Mr. Patella's impersonation of President Nixon before he noticed me and handed me his cup.

I left the pit and found Mary Beth in line at the snack bar. "You didn't wait for me, Nan. You never do."

"My Dad was waiting for me, but I'm finished now. I'll meet you on the wall." I was lightheaded from the Michelob I had guzzled. Draft beer served the best head.

Mary Beth arrived with a whole tray of stuff for us. The sodas spilled and made the hot dog rolls soggy. We sat on the wall that separated our club from The Blue Tip Shore Club and watched the crowd down at the snack bar. The tide was getting low, and I smelled the muscle beds. Here came Mom, walking real slow, her bob tied back in a scarf because she thought this made her look like Elizabeth Taylor. She and the actress seemed to be gaining weight at the same speed.

The great thing about our wall was that no one even looked over there; it was far enough away from everything. Gloria Gaynor played on the loudspeaker from next door, so we even had our own music. Over the wall was a rock pile where Mr. Fieldings collected his paperweights, and I could see splatterings of orange paint here and there.

"So, here's the plan," I said to Mary Beth, helping myself to her french fries. "And listen up because you have a key role. Without you, I can't catch them. At nine thirty tonight, when it gets dark, meet me behind the lifeguard shack under that tree. That's when they go in. Everybody else will be up at the clubhouse and they'll think they're safe. At nine forty-five we'll check for sounds, and if we hear them going at it, we'll follow through with Part Two of our plan."

"Then what?"

"Wait a minute. Wait a minute. Look over there," I said, fully inspired. There was my mother—her usual club soda and lime in one hand and a tuna salad sandwich in the other—with her girlfriends, the ones who gave Mrs. Fieldings the daggers. Up came Mr. Fieldings with his Ray Bans on and still a little wet from his swim—he swam religiously every day even in crummy weather. He headed directly to Mom, taking the soda from her hands so she didn't spill.

"Oh my god," said Mary Beth. "Go get your father. Now. He'll catch them talking."

"Big deal. Talking. What's that going to prove?"

"Well, I guess talking looks innocent. But, watch his thing. Maybe it'll rise up," she said, demonstrating with her finger.

We watched his thing.

Mary Beth knew more than I thought. Some of my friends were that way. You assumed they didn't know about any of that stuff, meanwhile they'd already been to second base.

"I know," Mary Beth said. Now she had my attention. "Maybe they're making a plan about tonight. Where to meet and all that."

"Yeah, right. With everyone standing around them." How was I going to count on Mary Beth tonight if she couldn't understand the workings of a basic cheap affair?

"Look, look," Mary Beth said with a new confidence. "Now they're alone."

Maybe Mom gave her friends the high sign and they left

them there to chat. Mom stood there, brazen with that tuna sandwich on the paper plate, her hips hidden under that long gauzy skirt. One thing my mother had that Mrs. Fieldings didn't have? Boobs. And, plenty of them. The cheaters stood there chatting, with my poor father right around the back of the snack bar, in the horseshoe pit, probably in a slump.

"Oooooooh," Mom yelled, and we jumped down from the wall with high expectations. Her pickle wedge fell in the sand and they both bent down to pick it up at the same time. Their heads banged. Mr. Fieldings' laugh was gargly from all those cigarettes.

I started to have my suspicions about this whole thing when Mom suddenly always had to get to the liquor store. My father would yell, "I better not catch you in there again, Chris. I better not find more empty bottles!" Stuff like that. But she didn't care; she'd go anyway. She even took me with her a few times, and I watched the love birds talk about wine. Mr. Fieldings would bring her a deep red bottle from the back of the store, and, with his cheek next to the label, they'd coo.

Now Mr. Fieldings pointed to an out-of-the-way snack table, and they both sat down. Seeing them together, sharing that sandwich, I couldn't concentrate on the second part of my plan. Mom put her thumb in her mouth and sucked off the tuna fish like she always did.

"Hey, Nan. NAN! You know, your mother looks exactly like Elizabeth Taylor. She's even got those eyes," Mary Beth said.

"Well, they're the same type, if you know what I mean."

That night, with the lifeguards off duty, Mary Beth and

I climbed up onto the lifeguard chair. From there, our float looked as untrustworthy as a rubber raft. The sun was going down, coloring the horizon salmon-pink, and the Good Year Blimp still hung in the same spot above us as it had all day like a bloated fish.

It was about eight thirty and the tide was nice and high now. Mary Beth was licking the salt off her arm. I realized then how much I would miss her. We were both going into seventh grade, but because I lived in New Rochelle and she lived in Yonkers, we never saw each other during the school year. Once Memorial Day came, we always picked right up where we had left off the year before.

We heard the theme from *The Godfather* playing over at Blue Tip.

"Oh, I loved that part!" Mary Beth was scanning the water's surface again.

"What part?"

"When Al Pacino marries the beautiful Italian girl? In Italy? I love Al Pacino. You see them do it on the bed. Then, he's always trying to teach her how to drive? And she really stinks? Then she goes out into the car one day, with a big smile, she kind of bops on the seat—she goes all by herself like she's going to surprise him? And the car blows up. Al Pacino flips out. Wants to kill everybody. It's so sad I can't stop thinking about it."

"You mean you actually see them do it? You see it go in? Wait a minute. How did *you* get to see it?"

"I went with my parents."

"They let you see that?"

Mary Beth stood up on the seat of the chair in her

rat-sighting stance, and I thought we were going to tip. "I see one! I see one! I told you!"

"Come on, let's go down. You go first. Go down backwards. Real slow."

When she reached the sand, I jumped from the third rung, feeling it in the ankle that I'd broken over the winter.

"I don't see any," I told her with a rock in my hand. "Besides, if they can make it all the way over here from Fort Slocum, we should put them on the swim team."

All I had to do was say I saw rats and I'd never get her to swim out to the float tonight. It had become our territory since the older kids lost interest in it. We were supposed to meet out on the float at nine fifty—after we caught Mom and Mr. Fieldings sucking it up in the cabana.

We roamed around the empty beach; the sand felt rocky underfoot and seemed to be getting rockier every summer. I wondered about all those pictures of turquoise water and powdery sand. Palm trees.

The pool was "L" shaped, the diving area in the short part, and tonight, the underwater bulbs were all lit. If anyone was sitting up in the blimp—although Mary Beth said it was run by remote control from a tower somewhere—they would look down and see a fat, neon L. The kiddy pool was fenced off and usually yellow by noon. Then there was a mountainous hill that rose and rose like the stomach of a gigantic bear sleeping on his back in the middle of Castaway Shore Club. At the top of the hill was our clubhouse, a wooden mansion, with huge picture windows and crooked floors, that used to be the home of one New Rochelle family in the old days, like the rest of the clubs that lined this strip. The clubhouse windows glowed, like the eyes, nose, and sour grin of a jack-o-lantern; the thunderous music of the live band drifted down to where we hid under the only tree on the beach, behind the lifeguard shack, where we made our plan.

"It's almost time," I said, holding a stick in my finger, puffing on it and squinting one-eyed, the way Mom smoked. "Chickening out?"

"No, it's just that, well, we already know what they're doing. So, then we're really not catching them, if we already know about it."

"Yeah, but Mom should know that someone knows and might tell Dad. Then she'll be scared."

"Your Mom seems nice, Nan. I mean, she's always nice to me."

"You're the one with the nice mother. You have a real mother. She even takes you to the movies. Trust me, OK? It's almost nine thirty."

In the dark, from under the tree, it was hard to see. The cabanas were little huts in the center of the beach; all of them were painted white because it was a club rule. Inside, you could do anything to them. The interior of the Fieldings' cabana was painted in a glossy orange that shimmered when they left their door propped open with a rock. Mary Beth's mother said all the orange all over the place was to draw attention to themselves. Of course, they had that Koi fish attached to a pole on top of their roof like no one else.

"You go to your lookout point by the pool fence. If you see anyone coming, bang on the corner pole with this oar—two times. At exactly nine forty on the pool clock, I will be done with my surprise attack. Everything will be over. Then go swim out to the float, and I'll meet you there."

"Why do we have to meet there? The water's so black now."

"Because no one can see us there. Just swim straight—not crooked. Depending on the way things go, I might be right behind you."

Mary Beth looked relieved. I could tell she was scared but I didn't know if she was scared about Mom, who she believed in, or about the swim out. Sometimes, in some weird way, I think she felt bad for me, when it was really I, who felt bad for her.

Just as it turned nine thirty, as if we had made the appointment ourselves for the couple meeting on the sly in the Fieldings' cabana, we could see a faint glow through the curtain. It was the only light on the beach we saw. Maybe there was a burning candle inside.

"Run to your post," I said.

I let a few moments pass and snuck up behind the row of huts. When I was sure they were in the cabana, I would bang on the door, yell "fire" with my disguised voice, and then run as fast as possible down to the water, dive in, and swim out to meet Mary Beth. They'd never know it was me. As I walked behind the huts, I noticed that the back window of the Fieldings' cabana was open. I saw the light and the faded orange curtain blowing through. It was funny how you could plan so carefully, and then something like this open window turned up like a gift.

My heart was pounding. I was going to catch Mom once and for all. The one good thing about sneaking around on the sand is that you don't make a sound. I was so intent on my mission, I forgot completely about Mary Beth.

It was almost nine forty. I wondered how so much time had passed already. I moved like a cat burglar and plastered myself between the Fieldings' cabana and the one next to it. I heard voices but I couldn't make out what they were saying. Then a silence. I moved against the wooden sides that felt cold now. I stood on my toes and looked through the corner of the window. The candle flickered wildly inside, making the walls jump with shapes and shadows. I heard an unfamiliar moan in a familiar voice. I looked around inside, distracted by the moving shadows on the wall, and finally found the heap of bodies on the floor. A man's broad, brown back, moving like gentle waves, with an anchor tattoo stamped above his white butt. Long, long legs of a woman tied around Dad's waist, and I recognized the next moan as the voice of Mrs. Fieldings.

I turned quickly, away from that view, and hit the sharp corner of the window frame. I ran away from them, listening to the wind of my breath. My chest pounded, and I found myself at the other end of the beach at the snack bar, all boarded up, the counter dirty with dried ketchup. Warm liquid dripped down my back, and slapping at my neck, I saw bright red blood on my hands. I carefully felt the back of my head, just now remembering the quick, sharp jab of the window frame. I pressed my head with my hand, afraid I would bleed to death from everything that was happening.

I went to the side door the servers used and, hiding behind the wall, smelled garbage, old chopped meat, and onion. A burning vomit rose in my throat and came out of my mouth in one wave. I kicked sand over it and realized that no one had a clue where I was, no one had followed me. I could die here. Even my father—my father!—and Mrs. Fieldings, who would never know I had been watching them.

I started back toward the beach. My head throbbed. I could see the clump of cabanas, the Fieldings' in the center, with that square of a window like one in a warm colonial house, slightly lit, the same as when I had left it.

I felt thick roots pushing into the soles of my feet. I concentrated, walking as quickly as I could to the pool fence. The clock said ten past ten. Mary Beth was not at her post. Of course not. Her job was done and she must have swum out to the float.

I moved my feet by lifting them with a sure but shaky strength, and made it down to the shoreline. I could hear the live band really rocking now, trying to sound like Eddie Kendricks. I put my feet in the water. How could the water have gotten so cold so fast? The freezing water on my bad ankle felt as if someone had hit it with a baseball bat. I waded in slowly, as I had so many times, happy times, when the water was just too cold to dive into. My bottom went numb when the water line got to my hips. I heard the loud and eerie sound of nothing.

The full moon cast a spotlight on the bare float. The only thing I saw was the black form of Fort Slocum, and I waved my hands wildly as if one of the tubular poles that jutted out would respond by reaching over to skim Mary Beth off the top of the water, wherever she might be.

I looked toward the area where she usually rested. Sometimes she played "dead man's float," where you lay in the water, face down, arms and legs slack. "M.B.," I called. "You are not going to believe this." I was crying. "M.B., I'm coming,

15

can you hear me? Do me a favor and answer me!" I waded in further, searching, and the ice water hit my chest and stopped my breath.

I imagined the rats coming to get me, hundreds of sneaky, quiet rats swimming just under the surface, their heads like so many bumps, coming straight at me. Then I felt rats around me, slick fatty rodents in the water with long tails whipping my skin, wiry tails wrapping around my stomach, pin teeth nibbling up and down my legs. They could smell my blood from the gash on my head. I could feel their teeth puncturing my skin for another drink and the cold water flushing into my body through the wounds they made.

I screamed and screamed, sobbing in-between. I heard a man yelling, "Nan, Nan is that you? What are you doing out there? Get out of there now." It was Dad, and he sounded angry. I also heard the distinctive voice of Mrs. Fieldings, yelling, "Sweetheart—you OK?" with the same baby doll voice she spoke to me at Bergdorf's, with the same voice she used with Dad. I turned around to see if they had clothes on. Dad was in his swimming trunks, and Mrs. Fieldings wore a short terry cloth robe, the belt dragging in the sand.

I met up with Dad on the shore and managed to tell him that Mary Beth was going to meet me out on the float. Now she wasn't there, at least I didn't think so.

"Oh my God," he said, pushing me out of the way as he dove in, swimming freestyle, his powerful kicks as loud as the entire swim team in a race. Every few feet he stopped and swam underwater. I guess he was looking for Mary Beth.

When he got to the float he climbed on top and stood, yelling to us through cupped hands. "Go for help—my God,

she's not here. Run for help. Call 911!" I could see the silhou-
ette of Dad's body, so much like the figure of Fort Slocum
behind him.

Mrs. Fieldings dragged me by the arm, talking to herself.
"This is terrible. Nanny—M.B. must be up in the clubhouse,
right? What did she tell you? Did she tell you where she was
going?"

We ran up the beach, past the pool, up the hill. I never
would have made it without Mrs. Fieldings pulling me by
the arm, although I really didn't want her to touch me. Mrs.
Fieldings was panting, locks of hair falling stylishly from her
French twist.

We entered the clubhouse through the side door, so we
stepped right into the party. No one even noticed us at first.
Mr. and Mrs. Patella were dancing alongside the teenagers.
On the last day of summer everyone partied together. There
was a buffet table set up against the entire wall for the Labor
Day "Neptune Feast" with cold cooked lobsters, in halves,
piled high. The desserts followed, and, at the very end of the
table, were deep tubs of ice cream.

Mrs. Fieldings ran to the front desk phone and left me
standing there in my bathing suit. I saw Mom at a cocktail
table near the window, her hair shining, sitting with another
couple. I walked through the smoky crowd in my Speedo;
maybe there was blood matted in my hair. When Mom caught
sight of me, she looked a little bewildered—you weren't allowed to enter the clubhouse in bathing suits.

I approached Mom's table and expected her to be angry
with me, the way I was dressed. Instead she looked happy to
see me. She waved at me to come sit with her, patted her own

lap to show me there was a seat. Mom was sitting with Mary Beth's parents, who looked happy, too, looking beyond me, expecting to see their daughter. Their two kind faces were so familiar to me; their expressions would stay with me forever.

I was still wet and sat down in the chair next to Mom. Fortunately, the band was so loud no one bothered to try to talk, so we all sat there and looked at each other, except Mom, her eyes on the dance floor, her shoulders going with the music. I wished she would throw her arms around me and press my face into her clean smell. But, I could see she was mesmerized by the rhythms she loved so much. Even at home she was always dancing around. I closed my eyes, and with all my concentration, tried to transform into a man. Then I would have asked Mom to dance. I imagined how happy she would be to finally have a partner. But as I looked down at my bare feet I knew it was impossible.

I used the next few moments to brace myself for what was to come and kept my eye on the doorway to the lobby. Mrs. Fieldings would burst through any second. I avoided looking at Mary Beth's parents and studied the room. The waitresses stood around with the vigilance of guards waiting to be called into action. The ceiling fans, now on their highest speed, looked wobbly, like they were about to fall and slice us all up. I would rather have been sliced than face my future. As I sat there, I noticed Mary Beth at the very end of the buffet table, in a sundress, the backs of her chunky arms bright pink, waiting patiently, as she was next in line to receive a cone.

# BLUE TIP SHORE CLUB

## New Year's Eve 1969

Dan-Dan the Shoe Man, as he was affectionately called, and his wife, Marie, had been members of the Blue Tip Shore Club for thirty-two years. Every New Year's Eve, Dan and Marie Cowley drove up the circular drive to the immense cherry doors of Blue Tip in their long swinging camel hair coats, and rang in the New Year with the midnight dance.

That New Year's of '69, Dan was melancholy. After all, another decade of his life was over. He was sixty now. And, Marie, well, she only made use of her personality after several Manhattans.

Dan sat alone with his gimlet, his noisemaker and the small dishes of half-eaten stuffed clams and bacon-wrapped shrimp, bitten and left behind. The picture windows around the room were sheets of black now. It was hard to believe there was a clear and peaceful view of the Long Island Sound beyond the icy night.

It was fifteen minutes till midnight, and a glaze had already formed on every car in the parking lot. Dan sat at his usual corner table, observing all the Versanis with high-high heels that Marie couldn't tolerate anymore. It was second nature to Dan, studying the familiar legs of all the female members, legs he had gently guided into so many shoes with the reverent touch of a holy man.

The women who came into Dan's store thought of nothing

else but shoes for those few moments. It was as if they checked their identities at the door before entering Dan's Shin Dig, free to slip in and out of one pair or another, as if it were a secret opportunity to try on fresh human skins. All it took was thirty steps around the perimeter of the store to become a different woman.

Dan was the man they offered themselves to at that moment. He was there to rid them of their doubts, to remind them they deserved to feel beautiful. More importantly, and this was apparent to Dan from the beginning, it gave them the freedom to feel whatever they wanted. He considered himself a doctor of sorts, administering care with a Gandhi-like generosity.

Years ago, when Dan first opened the store, he made a rule for himself: never date the customers. But, when Marie walked into Dan's Shin Dig for the first time, as slim as an extra-long cigarette, he was defenseless against his own rule. She headed straight for the sling-backs, scooped one up with her pinky and let the shoe dangle while she looked for a seat. Then, taking her sweet time, she sat down, shook off her alligator pumps, and summoned Dan by raising her toe.

Dan watched Marie as she left the leather-coated bar. She wore a gold cardboard hat splashed with glitter that had been handed out at the door when they arrived. She made her way to Dan, weaving relentlessly through the crowd even though her friends groped for her. She did not stop for Fay, whose laughter forced itself out of too much phlegm. Marie skimmed the edges of the dance floor with a drink held like a candle in front of her. Dan noticed Marie's legs were getting spindly, similar to the legs of Mr. Peanut, the figurine left behind by a toddler in his store that now sat rigidly on the cash register.

Dan wondered if his babying through the years contributed to her deterioration. Or, the booze. She was slipping away. The instinct to spoil his wife came from the warmest place inside of him. He wanted to take care of her, see pleasure on her delicate face.

It was Dan who cooked dinner every night when he arrived home from work, hoping Marie's appetite would pick up. Though Marie stopped at the market during the day, Dan mixed the drinks, set the table and grilled the steaks on their Weber, even in winter. He loved to barbeque on their fifteenth-floor patio—those were his moments—with a highball and tongs, infusing the air with the unmistakable smell of grilled beef as he kept an eye on his wife through the sliding-glass doors.

Dan moved further into the corner without leaving the table, listening to the ice hitting the windows in whip-lashing rhythms. He was constantly waving back to the other members who loved to be here on New Year's Eve—the most depressing of all holidays in his opinion—and they loved to chitchat, as if this were what life was all about. Worst of all were the cheerful resolutions. They were just bold reminders of things he would never do.

When Marie arrived at the table, her eyes resembled the two cherries at the bottom of her Manhattan. She plopped down across from her husband, kicked off one shoe, and wiggled her toes in his crotch. "Happy New Year's, Danny. It's almost time."

Dan felt himself harden. This was vintage Marie. The poke

of affection was a throwback of Marie's surprises in the old days. She use to hide nude in the stacks of shoe boxes so he could treat her (that was the way she put it) when he searched the stock room. He would find those long white legs sticking out of the stacks like falling signs, always dressed in knee-high suede boots, or spikes, depending on the season. When he returned to his customers his face was heated.

The waitress with the Irish brogue, whom Dan tipped generously at all the club events, traded his empty glass for a full one. Dan was eager for the burn of his drink.

Marie flung her hat on the table, her foot bouncing to the music. Her toes were a bit swollen. She had a corn that he sporadically cut off for her with his straight-edged razor, but it kept replacing itself. She stuffed her shoe back on, getting ready, and fooled with her freshly permed curls. For years, Marie had worn her bright blonde hair in a loose twist revealing the back of her neck that matched the color of buttermilk.

The lights were dimming and the Shane Fox Orchestra was getting silly, hamming it up and unbuttoning their vests that were too tight anyway. Shane's groggy voice smothered the mike. "Oooh baby, it's cold outside." He reminded the members that the roads were slick, so they might as well stay for a few rounds of coffee. No one was listening.

Dan said, "Looks like you're really at it tonight, hon. All that cheer."

He raised his glass to his wife, and, for a moment, saw her the way she used to be. He resented his memory for replacing this Marie with the younger one. When they first started dating she reminded Dan of the old cheesecake posters, with those legs and the cashmere sweaters. Her shoulders were almost broad and her posture erect which displayed her breasts in such a way that Dan viewed them as an extra bonus, a contribution to a relationship that was already a thing to admire.

"Oh," she waved her hand, dismissing Dan's suggestion that she was drinking too much. In fact, she was always whacking away his observations. "It is New Year's, for Christ's sake. Can't stand to be home when the ball hits at midnight, watching it drop on the tube. Everyone dancin' but me."

"Wait a minute." Dan corralled all previous holidays into a blurry picture. "Since when did we ever spend this night at home? We've been right here every year."

He studied the crystal chandeliers topped with serious seagulls, the gold-leaf chairs. A tremendous oil painting over the bar portrayed suspended ocean waves that might start rolling out of their frame any minute.

"Can't I enjoy myself tonight? Look—look at Fay and Chick," Marie said enviously, but not without admiration. "The Lindy is their forte."

"Fay's an ankle strap girl." Dan loved the new style with colored rhinestones that formed a T on the foot.

"Believe me, I'd be wearing them, if I could."

There was one problem. When Marie wore open shoes like those, it was difficult for Dan to pick up his wife's scent.

The drum roll got everybody up in a cult-like obedience, including Dan and Marie. A few old faithfuls still loitered at the bar. He ignored the wobbly feeling in his legs, took his wife's hand, and escorted her to the dance floor.

It was an unspoken rule with the men, and they joked about it every year. If they didn't grab their own wives at midnight, they'd be in deep shit. And, here was Marie, making sure she would have Dan for the final number.

They took their places on the wooden dance floor that still felt slippery after the pounding it had taken. The lights started to flicker; Dan figured there was an electrical problem due to the ice storm.

Shane started his orchestra so gently he looked like he was feeling something round and fragile in the air. The music melted into "My Funny Valentine," a song that made Marie cry.

Dan led Marie into the dance, and they found themselves close to Fay and Chick. Fay slid her foot toward Dan for his approval. "Festive," was all he managed to say, his voice more baritone than usual. Friends danced past, but Dan was not feeling sociable. He chalked it up to the New Year's blues. Marie's head felt lifeless in the crook of Dan's neck as he focused on the picture windows, trying to avoid knocking into the couples swirling around them.

After Marie stopped coming into the Dig to help out, Dan tried to imagine her days at home. He pictured her with her sugary black coffee and a cigarette, scanning *The New York Post* and the crossword puzzle, shaving her legs with his razor, arranging a bridge game with her friends. She had a mind for cards and could play for hours on end. Around five o'clock in the afternoons, he would be sure to find her on the couch reading the latest Harold Robbins.

Throughout the night he heard "Dan-Dan" in melodic bursts. He plastered a half smile on his face, so he would not have to talk to every Blue Tip member who called his name. A woman would grab his hand, press him tenderly in the chest, or lift her knee so that he could see, and approve, her formal shoe.

The countdown started. Marie clapped hard on each second, the noisemaker shoved into her velvet belt. Shane used a sparkling wand, conducting the last minute of 1969.

The floor's vibrations swam up Dan's legs. The members' faces reminded him of kid-style pancakes with embedded chocolate chip eyes, cherry noses and fat strips of whipped cream lips. He felt like he was going to fall.

Marie put her arm around his waist, and her head under his arm. "Danny," she said. "Gotcha."

Shouts of "Happy New Year!" traveled the room. The red-faced members blew their noisemakers and threw confetti.

Shane's guys kicked in with "Auld Lange Syne." Everyone clumped together, hugging and swaying. Marie let go of Dan for a moment, so she could toot her New Year's horn.

Dan held his wife close for the midnight dance, using her more as support than a dance partner. He pressed his hand on her back and moved her into the core of him, snug against his dampness. As he stepped into a gentle twirl, letting Marie glide under his heavy arm, he felt the floor rising up to his face.

"Let's go," he whispered in her ear.

She tilted her head in a "must we" expression, but let Dan lead the way.

At the coat-check, Dan and Marie waited patiently. They were the first to leave, so the girl made a fuss about finding their coats. Dan noticed the library doors were open; he had an urge to walk in and sit by the fire. The room was so dark you could barely make out the faces on the portraits lining the walls. The library seemed to belong to an estate somewhere in the English countryside, not here at Blue Tip.

Dan helped Marie with her coat. They seemed to shrink in full cuts that practically swept the floor, even Dan with his large frame.

The valet took forever to get the car; when he finally came into the lobby, his hair glistening, he warned the Cowleys that "it was an ice skating rink out there."

"Let's wait, Danny. What's the point?" Marie looped her hand under her husband's arm.

"Actually, we're better off leaving now. The roads will be less crowded."

Marie looked up the wide staircase that circled the clubhouse. "Remember?"

Dan remembered Francesca Barry's stilettos, but was surprised that Marie had brought it up. Perhaps it was the liquor. Or, she didn't want to go home and this was how she got back at him. Francesca, a striking but loud guest at a previous New Year's ball, had led him up those steps, pushed him through the first door they came to, and fell upon him, in a dark room filled with empty cartons and table linens. She had joked about his large body parts before pulling his nose down to where she'd wanted it to be.

Dan cringed, recalling how "should auld acquaintance be forgot..." had seeped under the doorway that night as he moved over her.

Dan was a slow and careful driver. The ride back to their

apartment in Larchmont wasn't long, but it might take an hour in this weather. He could not wait to be back in his own surroundings. He loved their building, a bit of old world in a quiet neighborhood. Dan had had the opportunity to go in as a partner and buy the building before real estate skyrocketed in Westchester, but he'd been afraid to take the chance. He wanted to kick himself in the ass every time he thought of the opportunity he'd let slip by.

Dan took the main roads with caution. He felt the back-end of his Caddy fishtail and wished he'd put sacks of sand in the trunk as he had been accustomed to doing every winter. He imagined he was flying, the tail of his car being held by a boy with a string.

Marie fiddled with the radio stations, then turned up the volume.

Guy Lombardo. This was the final, most depressing straw for Dan. He fantasized about sitting in his recliner in the living room that looked out on the balcony—his runway—where he often took off on a carpet ride into the empty, yet promising sky.

Dan gripped the wheel tightly, wondering how Marie could have fallen asleep between the sound of the radio and the sheer intensity of driving on ice. But then why should she worry, too?

Dan lightly tapped the gas pedal to keep his wheels rotating. He could see a car in his rearview mirror, the driver keeping his distance; Dan was grateful for his care. He couldn't make out a person behind the wheel, and thought perhaps it was a Dan-Dan mobile, carrying Dan's own conscience that would never stop following him around in 1970.

In fact, Dan felt he was the only one in the world. Dan and Guy Lombardo, together carting Dan's sleeping wife—his wife who now wore curls. He began to perspire and skillfully opened Marie's pocketbook with one hand to get a cigarette. He put one in his mouth and let it hang.

When Dan saw the long green awning of his building he felt a profound relief, as though an outstanding prayer had been answered. He pulled up to the entrance to let Marie out so she wouldn't have to walk too far.

"Honey, we're home," he said loudly over the music.

Marie plumped up her hair, half asleep. She unfastened her seat belt and buttoned her coat up to the neck.

"You go up and get in your cozies—and don't slip. You're not wearing your totes." Dan knew Marie would never be caught dead in totes with his business and all.

Too sleepy to operate her dry mouth, Marie patted her husband's hand. She let herself out of the car, slamming the door with all her strength, never noticing the bottom of her coat was caught.

Dan immediately put his foot on the gas pedal with his usual energy and the car began to swing back and forth like a woman's backside. He gave it more gas, feeling confident in the nearly empty parking lot, and the car took off in a full tailspin. He was on a joy ride and pressed the lighter on the dashboard so he could smoke his cigarette and ring in the New Year. In the safety of his own backyard, he finally felt in a party mood. It was his turn to have fun. The holiday was over and Dan was going to play a game with himself to celebrate.

He concentrated, trying to name the unfamiliar number.

It was Guy Lombardo all right, but what was the song? Dan took a deep drag off his cigarette, momentarily distracted by a thumping that sounded against the side of the car. He felt cheated. Now he actually felt the vibrations of an impact through his feet, but only for a moment and then it was gone.

Dan turned up the volume, finally recognizing the song, "Moonlight Becomes You." Lombardo did such a great job ruining the old standard that it had thrown him off. He parked his car in his assigned space, got out, and walked gingerly on the black ice. For a big man, he was light on his feet. Now he felt delightfully like a feather being pushed around by a brand new 1970 wind, without one resolution to contend with.

As Dan walked through the lot toward the apartment's entrance, he noticed a shoe, a woman's shoe, demure in the heel. He picked it up and brought it to his nose for its scent. It was Marie's shoe, no doubt about it. Dan's good nature returned as he realized his mind was playing tricks on him, as it had been all night. He held the shoe in his hand, truly believing it was a figment of his imagination, and flung it into the darkness as he waited for it to fall and slide into the New Year.

# TURQUOISE WATER
# BEHIND HIM

It was October, but Margo was still wearing short summer skirts. After letting herself in the front door, she walked through the sprawling horseshoe-shaped ranch house and down the curved hallway toward Paul's bedroom. She passed the dining room on the right, loaded with snakeskin pocketbooks, belts, leather pants and sweaters with studs. Pages ripped from *Vogue* and *Harper's Bazaar* were taped to the perimeter of the floor-length mirror. Boxes of chocolates, opened and tested, lay all over the dining room table.

On the buffet, under an oil painting of cypress trees, was a collection of elephants made of marble or glass, every trunk turned up in the same tight curl. The largest one in the middle of the herd was made of minty green wax, the kind of substance that glowed in the dark. Every time Margo snuck by the figures, she had to remind herself they were fake. Later, she learned that elephants with their trunks up like that were a sign of good luck.

Margo could smell the Desitin ointment and the menthol in the humidifier before she got to Paul's bedroom. Twisting her engagement ring to the inside of her hand, she walked in, and took a seat in the straight-backed chair at the foot of the bed. She swiftly kissed Paul on the cheek, knowing all too well that he was inhaling the smell of her as fast as he could.

"Look who's here," Richard, Paul's nurse, recited in an

Old Mother Hubbard way. He sat in the only chair in the room that could hold a man of his size. He had stopped reading aloud but left the granny-type glasses on the rounded tip of his nose. His uniform shirt was stiff with starch and stretched across his vast chest like a white tablecloth. You wouldn't dare call him 'Rich' or 'Richie.' When Paul's friends were brave enough to visit—some of them had kids in high school by now, which gave them a good excuse to scoot in and scoot out—they called him 'Richie' just to piss him off. His immense feet, in their perfectly clean white sneakers, rested on an ottoman shaped like an elephant.

"Richard, doesn't that thing belong in the other room?" Margo asked. "It gives me the creeps." She looked at Paul and laughed good-naturedly while Paul looked at Richard and laughed his own silent laugh. Richard went back to *The New York Times*.

Margo sat, not quite face to face with Paul. She felt aware of herself, the rise and fall of her chest taking in the air with all its additives, the zipper on her skirt digging into her skin, and, as always, a craving for a tall glass of water. She moved the chair closer to the bed.

She crossed and uncrossed her legs, listening to the pull and stick of her moist skin on the leather seat and feeling the glare of the clay statue of Padre Pio on the night table. It was cloaked in a swatch of brown velvet with kitchen string tied around its middle for a belt. These things, Margo knew, had been placed around the room by Paul's mom, Gabriella, who was more superstitious than Catholic.

Margo was wearing one of the sweaters Gabriella sold from her dining room table. The women who bought from her, the cha-chas with all the cash, were often in the dining room trying to squeeze their asses into buttery leather. The sweater Margo had on was a thin, purple cashmere with one strip of suede like half an "X" from the shoulder to the waist. The last time Margo visited, Gabriella had stuck it under her arm on her way out.

Paul started right up with the word game. It was as if the cork popped, but nothing came out except a rush of air. They had the game down to a science. Paul would shut his eyes for 'no,' blink for 'yes,' or just roll them around for frustration. He could stick out his tongue, and often did. When he smacked his lips together, over and over, it simply meant 'Margo.'

Margo was ready. "B—is it a B?"

Paul rolled his eyes.

"Give me a break," Margo joked, pressing her fingers to her temples, closing her eyes. "I need to get warmed up." She noticed how tightly the sheets were tucked in, hotel style, to keep Paul's body in place.

"C?" Margo guessed. "Hey, you be quiet over there. I can get this myself." Part of their fun when she was visiting was bossing Richard around.

Richard pretended to ignore them and picked up Paul's foot lotion, smearing it into his hands.

Behind Richard was a picture window—the kind that could not be opened— overlooking the mosaic-tiled pool in the backyard. Dead leaves all floated in the same direction, covering one end. Sometimes, the three would watch Gabriella in her leopard capris, skimming up the dead leaves, the way you would watch an exotic bird through glass in its own environment at the zoo. Margo admired Gabriella, doing the things she did at her age. Once, she had seen her up on a ladder, cleaning out the gutters on the south side of the roof. Gabriella bought the one-level house in Scarsdale after Paul's divorce, when he still had some movement in his legs. Pool therapy was recommended to build muscle.

Margo kept crossing and uncrossing her legs, shifting in her chair. She was fully infused with the hospital smells of the room, the taste of menthol in her mouth, the rest of her life temporarily gone. Sometimes, she just sat there, saying nothing, looking at Paul, Paul looking at her. How could this be? She often thought to herself as she smiled at him. She knew of other people who had multiple sclerosis, and they could move, or talk—say *something*—or roll themselves around in a wheel chair. Paul couldn't swat a fly off his nose.

Margo remembered meeting Paul for the first time, a couple of years ago, when shopping at Gabriella's. While her mother and Gabriella had chatted in the dining room, Margo, needing to use the phone, had pushed through the kitchen door. She found Paul sitting at the kitchen table in a wheel chair, riveted by a college football game on a small television, a bib tied around his neck. Richard was feeding him, scraping his chin with a spoon. When she'd said, *Hello,* she realized Paul couldn't answer. When Paul tried to communicate, she couldn't understand. Richard could and acted like the great translator. *Let me try,* she'd said, mostly to Richard. Now, however, she was a pro.

After meeting Paul that day, Margot had walked into the foyer, stunned. She recalled her mother mentioning Gabriella's heartbreak, and now that she had had a glimpse of it, she, too, felt she had fallen into a deep hole. She had noticed a photo of a young, healthy Paul in his bathing suit, with turquoise water behind him. He was leaning against a palm tree and looked as sculpted as the billboard models she saw in Times Square on her way to work. Gabriella had wanted her guests to see how her son used to be. Margot had folded her arms across her chest to make sure she was in control of her own body, instantly grateful.

Margo's father disapproved of her decision to visit Paul, convinced that she was torturing him in some way. What pissed Margo off more was her father's surprise at her kindness, his suspicion. *Why should a young woman like you go there and see that? And, you're engaged now for God sakes.*

Now, Paul stuck his tongue out at her.

"OK. Ready, sir." Margo straightened up.

Paul began his facial antics, tapping his tongue on his front teeth.

"Got it. L."

They were out of the gates and off. Richard let them play their game, probably knowing all along what Paul was trying to tell her. Paul blinked and blinked.

"I."

He made a *fuff* sound.

"F." Margo felt smug now.

Another reliable sound came from his mouth.

"T. The word is lift."

Margo took a break from the sentence. She wanted to rest on her laurels, having picked up the first word in record time. She wasn't about to make a guess now, gambling on the whole sentence. It was too early in the game.

34

"Where's Gabriella?" They both looked at Richard. He knew everything.

"She's in the city and going to stop at the A & P on the way home—she's making lasagna tonight."

Gabriella cooked easy-to-swallow meals, getting nutrition into her forty-four-year-old boy. Margo pictured Gabriella with her dangling earrings, driving to the train station in her Monte Carlo, an overflowing tote bag on the seat beside her.

As they sat there, the game well underway, Margo could feel something between Paul and Richard, some sort of secret. Sometimes, Margo and Paul left Richard out, and Richard didn't like that.

"All right, let's go." She called their attention, getting into position. "No, wait, I need something to drink. Paul? Anything?"

Paul was falling to the side, and Richard was already propping him up with more pillows. Once, he had been so tall and solid and broad shouldered, now he was a ladder falling. As Paul was being maneuvered, he looked at Margo as though she were abandoning him for a soda.

Margo wanted to let the air clear from whatever it was that hung between the two men. She got up slowly, her long blonde hair falling forward. She stood for several moments so Paul could look at her. He seemed to be studying her, filing away all the minute details of her image into his photographic memory.

Leaving the bedroom, Margo walked down the hall, through the dining room, and kicked off her shoes, taking note of a new shipment of leather jackets, before pushing through the swinging door into the kitchen. She felt a warm breeze, as if the herd of elephants were blowing their own noisy breath at her.

Breadcrumbs and parsley were scattered all over the counter, the food processor, plugged in and full of chopped onion. Miniature statues were placed on the stove, the way people stuck them on dashboards to ensure safe journeys.

Margo was searching in the fridge for a Diet Pepsi, when she noticed Richard behind her. He took the bottle from her hands and set it on the table. Then, he took her right hand and turned her engagement ring around to the outside, just as he had done the last few times she'd visited.

"You'll cut yourself that way."

"Well, what do you expect?"

"I expect you to tell him about Matthew. Today."

"You can call him 'Matt.' He wouldn't mind."

Margo searched the cabinet for a glass, while Richard stood behind her like a cop. Of course, she understood he was trying to get the news over and done with, but, he seemed annoyed that she was skipping out on them, running away with a normal plan that had fallen into her lap, and moving toward a normal life. She was grateful that Paul had Richard. He was able to lift the six-foot-three Paul in and out of the bathtub, in and out of the van, and onto the toilet bowl.

Margo worried that Richard might tell Paul about Matt before she did. They both knew it would upset him; he would assume that Margo would not visit so often. After the wedding, she would move into Matt's place in Manhattan and planned on being promoted to a new position, which would surely be more demanding of her time.

She tried to scan Richard's face without him noticing and

expected another scolding, but before he left the black-lac-quered kitchen, all he said was, "Don't leave your shoes in the dining room. One of the girls might take them."

Margo felt like a traitor, alone in the kitchen with her guilt and an old picture of Paul tacked to the bulletin board, wearing a tuxedo and a confident smile.

Forgetting her shoes, Margo helped herself to a piece of dark chocolate from an open box of candy in the dining room. A stone elephant, as big as a toy poodle, watched her from under the glass table. She glanced over the ripped-out magazine pages, a sloppy collage taped on the mirror; the models looked absent-minded and lucky. Margo recognized the pages. They had been torn from *Vogue*, whose offices were located in the same building as *Teen Idol*, where she was currently paying her dues as a research assistant for the "Fashion-Junkie" column. She envied the *Vogue* editors, who exuded the magazine's style—even when running through the lobby with their coffees and briefcases—and hoped to make her way onto their staff.

Margo walked back through the hallway in her bare feet, into the bedroom, ignoring Richard, who was again buried in his newspaper. She held her glass of Pepsi under Paul's chin as he bobbed for the straw. Her mouth close to his ear, she whispered, "Your friend was in there giving me some elephant lore." Settling back in her chair, she said, "OK, boss, I'm ready."

Margo saw, in the space between Paul's lips, a letter.

"U."

And then a "P" popping out. "P" was always a cinch. "Up. The word is up."

Richard was making plenty of noise with the newspaper, his head hidden behind the theater section. He went to see everything on Broadway. Margo stuck her tongue out at him, and Paul laughed. Now it was Margo and Paul against Richard.

Paul kept eyeing the tissue box. This was the other ritual, getting all sweaty in the game like athletes. Margo was perspiring, and he wanted her to take a tissue and wipe her forehead, the bridge of her nose, her mouth, which she did. She then took the damp tissue and kneeled on the floor next to him. She pulled his fingers back and wiped the moisture collected in his lifelines, his sweat mixing with hers. Sometimes, when she pulled Paul's fingers away from his palm, there would be a slight yeast odor, but she could only smell it if she got close. She didn't care if she was annoying Richard, who kept Paul's body as immaculate as he kept his own.

Margot returned to her chair. "Next letter," she said weakly. She knew it would be a difficult one. It always happened like that. She'd be on a streak then get dead stuck. She sat still, a good student, observing Paul's mouth. His lips were full and never dry like her own were at the moment. Sometimes, she groped hard for a letter, as if the alphabet were strung between them. She felt, too, that if she concentrated hard enough, she would be able to read his mind.

He was still performing letters with the only movable part of his body.

"Y—Y?"

He was getting anxious and had already moved on to the next clue.

"O?"

"U?"

"R?"

Richard folded his newspaper into his lap. He thought only he could understand his patient.

The doorbell rang again and again.

"Must be one of the girls," Richard said. "Now I'm going to miss the best part of the show."

One of the cha-chas was there to pick up her order, so Richard pitched in. He didn't seem to mind. Gabriella wouldn't be back for hours. The only thing she ever did was go grocery shopping, or to the beauty parlor, and to the bank. Today, however, she had gone to Seventh Avenue in New York to the houses she ordered from. Most of the clothes came to her U.P.S.

Margo heard the lavish talk and jingles going on between Richard and Gabriella's customer. Whoever was at the door was delighted to see Richard.

Relieved to be alone, not that Richard ever presided over them, they were happy for the moment. Margo felt her diamond ring against her bare leg.

Paul hissed.

"S."

Paul exhaled.

"H."

Paul winked.

"I."

Paul chewed.

"R."

The old reliable "T" sound came from Paul's mouth in a hurry. He was perspiring.

*Shirt*, Margo said to herself. *Lift up your shirt.* She let it sink in, while she focused on a small plastic hose attached to a box on the night table. She had seen Paul blow into the hose, making the ball inside the box flutter up and down. Two years of religiously visiting him, each visit now stuck in her chest, swelling, so that she was forced to examine what had really happened. Now, she couldn't deliver, and he would feel punished for it. Margo, afraid to look, felt Paul waiting. Perhaps she misunderstood the letters.

She managed, "Lift up my shirt?"

The words rose around them.

Richard rushed in, peach lipstick on each cheek. He was carrying a ceramic elephant one of Gabriella's customers brought home from Florence. She could tell by the way he looked at them, he knew the game was over. He put the elephant down on the rug near the bed and maneuvered Paul's body by pulling the sheets and pillows under him so that he was again straight and comfortable.

Margo tried not to watch this ritual—it had to be embarrassing—and stared down at the new elephant in bright Florentine colors. His trunk, resting over a tusk, looked bloated and heavy.

Richard appeared to be getting Paul ready for something, and now, Margo felt like the one left out. Richard propped Paul upright, combed his hair, and placed a little towel roll behind his neck so his head wouldn't flop. Deftly, with a lemony swab, he cleaned out Paul's mouth so fast that Margo wasn't even sure he had done it.

During all this, the sentence—*Lift up your shirt*—played in Margo's head. She felt the urge to say it aloud, to see the expression on Richard's face, but she also felt ashamed. It might upset Paul, and Richard didn't deserve that either.

Richard folded Paul's hands together over his shapeless stomach, finished his duties, and stood straight, his head almost to the ceiling, a good giant finished with his deeds, leaving the fairies to play. He gave Margo one of his famous looks, glared down at her ring finger as a reminder, and left the room, closing the door firmly to make his point.

"Lipstick," Margo whispered. "All over him." She dotted her face with her finger. "The one with the bracelets did it. Big Boy didn't stand a chance."

Paul didn't laugh. He was fresh, combed, and ready.

Margo played out the words she would say in her mind. *Paul—if you knew Matt, you'd like him. If you don't like him, he's history.* She'd make a joke of it.

Margo saw letters all over Paul's face, jumbled up, desperate. He was starting again with the L, the I, the F, the T. She thought of the game she had played in secret the night before, at a dinner with Matt and his law partners. Pretending she was deaf, she had studied Matt's mouth as he chatted to a lawyer. She couldn't pick up a signal there, so she searched the rest of Matt's face for clues, his gesturing hands, and his body, hunched into the conversation. Finally, she gave up. She hadn't given it a second thought. Until now.

Margo got out of her chair, the back of her knees wet, her hands so moist her engagement ring slipped. She opened her mouth and thought about the place inside her where her voice began. She imagined a hollow black box deep within her throat, the top lid propped open. Nothing emerged; she could not form a single word.

Her sudden paralysis made everything in the room come to life. She felt the presence of Jesus Christ in the portrait above Paul's head, staring past them, uninvolved. The Padre Pio statue held his hand up like a crossing guard. There was a pile of untouched magazines—*Forbes, Fortune, Business Week*—the covers alive with functioning executives in suits. The humidifier hissed, the smell of menthol coated her with another layer.

On that too-warm day in mid-October, no one watched Margo from the backyard, through the picture window, and she looked out on the scene that would be her audience—Gabriella's ghosts and scarecrows, which she must have pulled from the shed and were now huddled together, as dead leaves accumulated in the pool.

Margot thought of all of Paul's friends who stopped visiting because they couldn't handle it. She could hear her father's demanding voice, forbidding her to see a sick man, and she could see the warning expression in Richard's eyes.

And, Paul's wife. She left him when he could no longer tie his shoes.

Margo lifted her sweater up and over her head. She put her hands behind her back, pulled off her ring, letting it drop into the rug, and unfastened the hooks of her bra. She slipped off her skirt, and then her underwear, with one finger, down to the floor.

She looked down at herself, at the sweat on her breasts, at her toes half-hidden in the thick, soft rug. Paul's breathing was labored, and Margo looked around the room for the contraption Richard used when Paul got like this. But he never got like this exactly.

Paul's mouth began to form letters, but he stopped. His eyes softened. It seemed as though this was what he had wanted. It wasn't too much to ask. Margo saw Paul's beautiful white teeth and remembered the photo of him in his tuxedo, and the one where he wore his bathing suit with the turquoise ocean behind him.

Paul pushed his chin out with all his might, moisture gathering in the corners of his mouth. As Margo moved closer, she almost knocked down the cold ceramic elephant. She continued on, feeling the weight of Paul's need on her, moving through this secretive, shameful game. She got on the tight sheets of the bed, carefully positioning herself so that she was face to face with Paul, her legs on each side of him.

She pulled back his fingers and opened his hands.

# IN THE BEACH CHAIR

The crowd at Holy Sepulcher Cemetery had no order or shape, just pockets of space here and there as if the sun were burning holes through the mass, completely missing two tall targets, Stef and her mother, Constance. Stef noticed the heat made her mother's unworldly pink lipstick seep upwards and outwards into the lines around her mouth, a frame of sorts for the word "dirt," the word her mother kept whispering to her all through the service. And wouldn't it be hilarious if it was plain old dirt that would make her mother forget all the shit that had gone back and forth between her and her sister Linnie before she'd died?

"Look at the dirt," Constance said again, her face crunched up like she had a sour ball under her tongue.

Stef looked around, creeped out by the fresh mounds nearby.

"There's a seam." And in the palm of her hand, her mother drew the seam that went down the center of the coffin, her thick gold ring with the diamond strip all around distracting Stef. She adored the ring and her mother waved it in front of her as often as she could.

Constance was on a soft-spoken tirade. "Must be made of goddamn fiberglass," she said, looking over the heads in front of them. "That's what the bastard bought," referring to Aunt Linnie's born-again Christian husband.

The pall bearers threw fistfuls of dirt over the coffin while

Father Boyle stood over to the side, reading from his prayer book like he knew anything about love, human love. The dirt, Constance insisted, was getting stuck in the seam, and surely the dirt was falling in through the crack and onto her sister (who'd died like a rabbit under the porch) over her deflated stomach, over the only decent dress she ever had, one that Constance had bought for this occasion.

Stef figured her mother would have sprung for the coffin, too, to spread some butter over her guilt, but Uncle Jeff wanted to buy it himself with his own five hundred bucks, so everyone would feel sorry for him.

Constance reached for the candies in her purse, a sign that meant she was turning over an irritating situation in her mind.

"You know what that bastard said to me this morning with my poor dead sister in the same room?" Constance pulled the skin above her daughter's elbow. "Steffie has become a woman. She could rival my wife—before the boys, before the lymphoma."

"Since when do you give a shit what he says," Stef said in her usual under-the-breath response, trying to recover from how her mother referred to Aunt Linnie—my *poor* dead sister—like she was all heart.

It was clear to Stef that her mother wasn't passing on a compliment. This was a warning. Stef couldn't see any similarity between herself—tall and broad with straight black hair—and the Northern Italian colors of her mother's family. It was nice to feel her mother studying her at that moment, affectionately rearranging her hair behind her shoulders, gazing at her slender nose, her full cheeks, even if she was only searching for the reference Uncle Jeff had made.

Stef had had no contact with the Olsens for five years now, because of the various silent treatments inflicted by both sides. But as she imagined Aunt Linnie lying in the fiberglass box, her rust-colored curls still plump because hair, they say, doesn't die, Stef knew she should be there.

Constance shoved her purse into her daughter's hands, her breath full of butterscotch. "My baby sister," she said and moved toward the coffin.

Stef felt ridiculous, holding two purses, one of them clearly old ladyish, so fat with used tissues and mess inside, all smelling of Madam Rochas perfume, even the candy. Stef found one of the gooey Lifesavers in her mother's purse, and watched as her mother twisted her large body from one side to the other, squeezing through the crowd, putting a hand gently on a shoulder or an arm as she passed. Stef saw the guilt, all ribbony and flowing down her back like the tails of an Easter hat.

Constance wore a classic black suit with white piping and Stef tried to picture her mother at her own father's funeral, when Stef was only five like her cousin Tommy was now. Had Constance carried on about something then? Had she truly been thin, the way she'd described herself? When she used to put Stef to bed as a child, Constance had often told her the story of her dad's funeral, how the pallbearers could hardly carry a man of his size on their shoulders. Constance had worried they'd drop the hand-finished oak casket, with the creamy taffeta interior, pop the seal, and her husband would roll out onto the hardened soil like the trunk of an oak tree, his eyes unglued and staring straight ahead.

She'd told her daughter it was the *what-ifs* in life that would kill her.

Stef couldn't remember a thing about that day, so she inserted the image of her father falling and rolling on the ground.

Stef had been away at boarding school when she got the news about Aunt Linnie, but from what she'd gathered through her mother's too-busy-to-talk phone calls, her mother had been by Linnie's side over the past year. Constance had temporarily closed her shop—not that she'd ever had normal business hours anyway—and gone back to her sister because of the cancer, the cancer she had fully expected. Aunt Linnie, the beautiful one, had just turned forty, and she was the first to go, summoned up, no doubt, by their dead mother. Aunt Linnie had been Grandma Dottie's favorite. She was everybody's favorite, except, maybe, Uncle Jeff's.

Four bright blonde heads kept turning back in Stef's direction, even Tommy, with shocking colors around their necks—pinks, neon greens, oranges—like surfer boys, their clothes bagging on them.

Stef had never gotten this kind of attention from the Olsen boys before. She felt like a giant in her black sheath dress, kitten heels, and two purses, overlooking the townspeople, her eye on one troublemaker in particular. Away at school, she had never had this feeling, that creeping sense that something could go wrong any minute.

She watched as her mother moved closer to the coffin, and Father Boyle looked up from his prayer book. Was it her mother that distracted him, or, did the clouds remind him of the whipped cream that would soon be floating on top of his Irish coffee? That must be how priests got off, Stef thought, if they weren't helping themselves to young boys.

Stef noticed her mother's hair, fried from all the bleach, was becoming undone from her usual chignon as she made it up to the coffin and stood in front of it like a soldier too tired to salute.

Father Boyle continued talking about Linnie's disposition throughout her illness; her dedication to education in the town of Pelham where Jeff Olson was now teaching eighth grade math over at the high school. Of course, Father never mentioned why everyone just wanted to shake her sometimes.

The expression drained out of his words when he looked over to Constance.

Uncle Jeff left his spot in the front row and approached Stef's mom with a secret-service gait, his body aging into the shape of an extra-large egg, wearing the same Aviator type sunglasses on the sunken bridge of his nose like he always wore. He stood at the side, his hands behind his back.

Her mother made the sign of the cross, and Stef was relieved. People will think she is distraught and will understand the gesture.

The gesture grew.

Constance raised her foot and placed the pointy toe of her shoe against the casket. Not kicking, exactly. Pressing. Tapping. A wake-up-sleepy-head kind of a tap.

Stef could barely stand; the heat and embarrassment penetrated her from all angles. All she could do was watch her mother's bloated calf, in its silvery stocking, catching the sunlight like the scales on a striped bass.

The oldest Olsen, two years older than Stef, left his seat, practically ran over to Constance, and offered her his elbow. This was going to be good. She'd flip him on his ass, the mood she was in.

As Stef watched the exchanges between her cousin and her mother, the whispers, the offering of a tissue, she felt that old jealousy ream through her. She observed the joy in her mother's face, like a goddamn proud grandmother, taking the nineteen-year-old boy's skinny arm like the staff of some annoying teen god.

He calmed her mother. Stef could barely stand, watching her mother rest her head on the boy's shoulder after he escorted her to a seat in the front row.

After the service, still in her seat, her own aggravation swimming, Stef shook her mother's purse and listened for the sound of car keys, so she wouldn't have to put her hand in there. She hadn't had much practice driving, being away at boarding school—she had been into it more before she got her license. The thought of driving her mother's boat of a car in the funeral procession back to the Olsen house was just boring.

Stef walked over the lawn, carefully stepping around the vibrations of the souls buried six feet under, to the car parked far from the others. In the car, she took off her shoes, turned up the radio and the AC, and got in the line of traffic waiting to leave the cemetery. The two purses sat on the passenger seat.

Constance was being helped into the family limousine.

When Stef arrived at the Olsen house, Tommy was outside on the swing set. He was towheaded like the rest of them. She could stare at him forever, playing in his world, astonished that he was the baby she once held in her arms. She envisioned picking him up, holding him, ignoring her mother and the rest, and taking him for a ride in the car. She walked to him, one of the candies in her hand. "Hey, big T.J. Olsen. Remember me? Steffie? Bet you don't!" She stooped down, her strong legs almost ripping the seams of her dress. He looked at her and ran into a hut in the corner of his play area.

Inside the Olsen house, Stef recognized the chandelier in the dining room, visible from the front door. It was from her mother's shop and used to hang in the Confederate section, a row of small gold eagles perched around the rim of its top tier. And, there was her mother, the light from above hitting her sparkly ring, handing out punch in plastic cups.

The house was unusual for this part of Pelham, with its roominess and parquet floors. Grandma Dottie had bought the house for them, but the Olsens couldn't afford the up-keep. The oldest Olsen, the ever annoying, spotted her and waved, acting less confident than he had handling her mother. She pointed upstairs, signaling she had to use the bathroom. She saw Aunt Linnie's slippers on the bottom step.

There was nothing more scary than seeing the shoes of a dead person.

Stef walked up the stairway barefoot, the sisal rug hurting her feet like when she was eleven, the last time she was in the house. Her mother had sent her, with a present, to take care of Aunt Linnie right after Tommy had been born. Aunt Linnie had been perfectly healthy then, just tired from another baby, and Uncle Jeff had been distracted with his new carpet business.

With the noise of the party growing underneath her, Stef opened the door, walked into the dark room, and sat on the edge of the unmade bed and remembered that day.

*Each one of Aunt Linnie's babies had looked the same to Steffie, blue-veined, chickeny, and bald with an indentation on top of their heads as if they were branded to a race on a pileless, densely patterned planet. But they belonged to Uncle Jeff, all with the same visible rims of white around each eyeball, eyes protruding, like they were surprised to find you, or surprised that you had found them.*

*Steffie had walked up the steps to the second floor with her dead grandmother's jewelry box, holding it with the tips of her fingers so nothing would rub off on her. Her mother had instructed her to give the gift to Linnie, she wanted it out of the house, and had said, "Just like my mother to leave it here for one of us to inherit. I'll be damned if I'm going to be the one to end up with the swollen belly and the cancer look in my eyes."*

*Steffie had pictured the disease under the pearl inlays as gray spotted wafers. She placed the box on the dresser in Aunt Linnie's bedroom, far from the bed, close to Uncle Jeff's can of deodorant.*

*Downstairs, Jeff Olsen had been laying a rug in the living room, punching a tool with his knee to stretch the carpet so that it would lay flat against the floor. He dropped the tool, kicked it in, in a drop-kick, drop-kick rhythm, stapling around the perimeter of the room. Steffie had felt the vibrations. Her uncle had owned Olsen's Carpets for a short period of time, and every room, including the kitchen and bathrooms were now covered, filling the house with its own fibrous smell under funky layers of milk, kitchen drippings, and urine from the bathroom toilets that were just-missed targets for the boys.*

*Uncle Jeff had called up to her in his pleading voice (he and Aunt Linnie had all kinds of voices they used with each other, depending on the fluctuating moods of their relationship, and, at the very least, attached the diminutive "y" sound to everyone's name). "Make sure she eats her sandwich. Please. Then let her get some sleep. Tommy had her up all night."*

*Steffie had pushed off her sneakers so she could feel the new multi-colored shag rug in the bedroom, the only carpet in the house you could hide your toes in, when she entered Aunt Linnie's bedroom.*

*Linnie had been in bed and her petite milky arm lay over her face, her hair free from her usual messy bun, her small curls filling the space between her head and shoulders like low unruly bushes, burnt from too much sun.*

*"Steffie, baby," she'd said in her little girl voice, and Stef had been surprised she couldn't e-nun-ci-ate better. Any teacher would have made her repeat herself. "Come here."*

*She'd reached for her aunt's hand.*

*"No, no, baby, here. This hand."*

*Stef had wondered how her aunt knew it was her niece, with her face still covered.*

*"How's my only girl?" which was how her aunt had always referred to her. "I wish your daddy had gotten a chance to enjoy you. You remember him?"*

*When Stef thought about her father, it was like seeing him, and that would make her dead, too. She closed her eyes. Floating. Driving in his leathery-smelling Caddy, so smooth, floating like a Cabin Cruiser over the neighborhood streets. The smoke shop. Taking the paper rings off his Antonio Cleopatra cigars and putting them on her fingers.*

*"Your Daddy helped me." Aunt Linny squeezed Stef's hand intermittently until she fell asleep.*

*Stef had tried to think back, tried to think of her dad and Aunt Linnie, and how he had helped her. Nothing came to her really, except sitting behind them in his car, Aunt Linnie in the passenger seat. Taking her away.*

*Then the coffin popping open, Dad rolling on the ground. Did he hurt his head?*

*She noticed the untouched sandwich on Daffodil bread with the American cheese that was always in the Olsen's fridge without a wrapper. An empty pitcher and paper cup on its side. Just then she remembered more instructions from her mother.*

*"Make sure she always has fresh water so she can keep up with the milk."*

*The baby's cry was sudden and by reflex Stef squeezed her aunt's hand too hard, but she didn't budge. The basinet was on the far side of the large bedroom that was nearly empty, half in, half out of the closet.*

*She couldn't wait another minute to see and hold Tommy. She could already smell the baby powder. So much better than a doll, a warm wiggler in her arms.*

*Steffie stood up and the arm that covered Linnie's face fell to the side. She didn't recognize her aunt's mouth, so thick and plum colored. She followed the trail of red dots, some kind of rash or burn, to her swollen cheek. Stef had knelt next to the bed, unable to move, longing to take Linnie's hand again. The baby continued to wail and for a moment Steffie thought it must be her aunt, she must be the one crying.*

Stef turned away from the worn, thin pillows. She sat on the sheets where her aunt's small feet must have been just a few days ago. For a moment, she imagined her, laying in the bed, her eyes embedded deep in her pudding face, her skin draped over her bones, her belly as swollen as when she was pregnant with Tommy. "Come here, baby, come to me."

Stef quickly got off the bed, trying not to inhale. The cancer cells were floating, falling, melting into her skin. She backed up toward the door, planning to shower at home with the Betadine soap, and saw the jewelry box on the dresser, sitting in the middle of Aunt Linnie's perfume bottles.

"Mom's the one that should have come to you," Stef said aloud to the image in the bed. She could feel her insides being pulled into a drain. If she hadn't brought the box to her aunt, Linnie wouldn't have inherited the cancer from Grandma Dottie. Stef had known what was in the box and she'd brought it anyway. She did what her mother told her and now Linnie was dead.

Before Stef left the room, she picked up a pencil and used it to lift the top of the box. It was so stuffed with bills and papers and prayer cards that it didn't close. As she held the top open, a loose, pearl inlay slid off and fell on the dresser with a *click*. Wrapping her hand in a tissue, Stef picked it up and folded the tissue around it. Stef left the room, eyeing her mother's purse just outside the door, and slipped the pearl inlay in the side pocket next to her mother's Lifesavers.

Stef crept down the stairway and partially saw the round, robed figure of Father Boyle. Light reflecting off his shiny head, he held a dish of cheesecake in his hand. He was talking, shaking his fork. The priest turned everything into some fucking sick parable: "After they got the diagnosis, they pulled over on the side of the road and held each other. Jeff Olsen promised his Linnie right then and there he was going to change his ways. This wasn't bad news. No. This was a *rebirth*." Wasn't bad news?

Stef had heard enough and needed to get out before Father

Boyle tacked on his morbid clincher, the ones he was famous for that made everyone go silent. And what the hell did he know? Being taken care of in the rectory had to be easier than worrying about your own family. And, God only knew the sick shit he might get into on his own.

Stef went around the staircase, walked out onto the porch in the back of the house. There was an old rocker in the corner, and she sat down in it, her face and neck moist from wanting to escape, her pearl necklace too heavy.

"That's Mommy's chair," Tommy popped up. Blue stains from a snow cone decorated his small bare chest.

"Oh, I wouldn't want to sit on Mommy's chair. I really don't, Tommy." Stef jumped up. "Wanna play?"

"Play what?"

"A game."

"OK."

"Is my mom in the house?" Stef asked, so could keep her distance.

"Aunt Connie?"

"Yes."

"Guess so."

"Where should we play?" Stef looked around the backyard, the chrome on the bikes shining dangerously hot. Two beach balls smelled like hot plastic. Of course, the Olsen's balls were deflated.

"Under the porch."

"Isn't it gross down there? I have a dress on. Whatever." Stef got up and followed Tommy down the steps to the opening at the base of the house, its wooden slats kicked in. Crawling in behind him, the jagged wood scraped her arms.

When they were in his space, she immediately felt a layer of coolness slip over her.

Beneath the house, Tommy could stand, but Stef had to stoop. She was surprised to find a spacious playroom with a dirt floor matted from all of Tommy's running and rolls of old carpet piled to the sides like bleachers. The space smelled of rich soil, mildew, and faintly of urine. She worried there might be mice nesting in the abandoned old couch, or worse. Small squares of carpet samples marked off different sections: jail, corral. A beach chair, half empty of its plastic strips, reclined near Tommy's stockpile of plastic artillery and glass bottles.

"I'm a gorilla," Stef growled, pushing out her chin, but he was unappreciative.

He picked up a rubber Bowie knife and shoved it in his front pocket. She hoped he was just showing off for her.

"So this is where you cousins are hiding!" Uncle Jeff was stuffing himself through the opening, his jowls a little forward in that position. When he was able to slightly straighten up, his hand went deep in his pocket to jingle his change. Stef had forgotten about that noise of his.

"You showing your all-grown-up cousin your saloon? Tommy doesn't allow too many down here, Steffie. You must be a special pardner."

"I can barely get him to speak to me," Stef replied, without looking at her uncle. She could always do without his eye contact.

"The only other lady allowed down here was his mom. Can I stay, T.J?" Uncle Jeff was already looking for a spot to sit his fat ass.

"Guess so."

"Maybe I should go see if mom needs help up there," Stef said. She'd prefer her mother's antics over being in the same saloon with her Uncle.

"Oh, you know your mom. She's taking control. Besides, I think you have an admirer."

Tommy was pointing to the lounge chair, so she carefully sat herself in it. He was warming up and she wasn't going to ruin it. With her bare feet and legs extended in front of her, Stef was careful to keep her short dress tucked tightly about her legs. She watched her uncle shuffling around like the Hunchback of Notre Dame.

Stef had forgotten how depressing they all were—except for T.J. Or, she had never realized how depressing they were until now, freshly back from St. James boarding school, where everything, even the silverware in the cafeteria, seemed steeped in some kind of proud one-hundred-and-fifty-year-old history. Her school friends, whom she knew only casually, were all connected to legacies she was only beginning to understand. What she did understand, however, was that her own heritage was far from illustrious.

A flash feeling of Mr. Porter. Watching him lecture.

Stef loved doing crew, the pull in her core, being out on the water, where she remembered her Dad, and how they used to fish in a rowboat on Long Island Sound. They had cast for flounder not far from the shore. Her father, massive in bulk, hunched over the hook and bait, yet she had been proud to be able to dip the oars in the water and pull him around.

It was a relief, walking through the wild and wooded areas

on campus; taking a run around Blue Hill Pond, heated in the winters, where she could see the ancient koi fish; slapping the feet of the massive stone dogs of Oliver Hall as she ran by; finishing up with calve stretches against the Scholar tree. She worked hard, so afraid that she would fail and be sent home to Pelham High School to live with her mother. Her father's will had stipulated that she attend Saint James. Her mother referred to it as "the school with the first squash courts in America. That's the country club my daughter belongs to!" The kids at Saint James were nothing like the kids at Pelham, and not even close to the kids on planet Olsen.

Stef had often wondered why her father had insisted on her attending that particular school; he had not gone there himself. It made Stef love him more.

Lying in the beach chair, she felt the presence of Aunt Linnie, her girliness, the way her small hand had reached for Stef's, how she'd held Stef's hand and walked down the wide Olsen hallway, down to the kitchen, and held it even while opening the fridge. *My only girl needs a snack doodle.* For a moment, there under the porch, Stef felt Aunt Linnie's hand in hers, as if now Linnie's hand was the hand of a child.

*My only girl.*

Uncle Jeff deposited a pile of rug mats near Stef's chair and sat awkwardly on top of them, his face close to Stef's bare feet. He inhaled deeply as if he was trying to smell her toes, his protruding eyes so visible in the dim light.

"I'd give my right arm to teach at an institution like the one you're at. You don't know how lucky you are, Steffie, the exposure. You've been blessed. You know, you look like one of those students."

*Blessed.* "What do you mean?"

"Oh, there's a look. A tone of voice."

Tommy held out his two small palms, offering Stef three red-tipped plastic bullets.

"Thank you. Can I keep them for my gun?"

"Use them on the trail. Apaches," Tommy replied, solemnly.

"I will. I will take them back to school with me. You never know. I run in the woods."

Stef described everything she saw on her runs. Uncle Jeff listened intently, too, staring, as if she were talking to him. Stef felt a quiet thrill, being accepted by Tommy, and it was all she could do not to grab him, to press his face into hers, and spoil it. At the same time, she felt the weight of her own memories press on her cheek.

*The rug burns on Aunt Linnie's face.*

Stef wanted to ask Uncle Jeff about it, but the question choked her before she got to it.

"What's wrong," he asked, as if he were the kindest man in the world.

"Just thinking." She could not stop the tears, and certainly didn't want Tommy to see.

"She was so disappointed that you didn't come when she asked. She was—well, there's no point now."

"Asked?"

"Oh, come on now. You know. But she figured you were at your ritzy school. And you know how she was about grades."

"I didn't know."

"You ignored her message."

"What message?"

"Linnie left word many times, through Constance. She had something she wanted to give you."

Jeff Olsen put his hand on Stef's ankle, and she pulled her leg away from him.

He stared up, into her crotch. She could feel his glare seeping into her.

The sound of Constance's crackly voice interrupted them. A familiar, torturous moan.

Tommy, his little body half-in and half-out of the opening, was pulling his aunt under the porch. Constance didn't like bending; her suit jacket was off and left somewhere, her blouse pulled out and hung over her middle.

"Steffie, Steffie get out of the chair. Now. What the hell are you doing, Jeff Olsen, putting my daughter in the chair my sister died in?" She made it over with some difficulty and pulled her daughter from the chair, brushing the dirt from the back of her dress, her long arms, and the back of her head. "Oh no, they aren't going to take you, too," Constance mumbled under her breath, the one way she and her daughter were alike.

"Why didn't you tell me? Why didn't you tell me Aunt Linnie wanted to see me before she died, Mom?" The rage had crept around and hardened the ridge of her nose.

Tommy was running as fast as he could around the perimeter of the area.

"She laid under this house, for two days, and no one knew she was here. Dead." Constance said in a slow and rising rhythm.

"Tommy knew, Steffie, he just didn't tell anyone where she was. He wanted to keep his mother. We never thought to look here, didn't even know how she had the strength to get under here."

Jeff Olsen was crying, his hands over his face, and Steffie, in this one instance, believed he was sincere.

Tommy dove through the opening and ran out into the sun.

"I would have come, Mom."

"Yeah? Well, my sister wanted to give you the box, and I didn't want her to give it to you."

Stef felt her mother studying her and didn't know whether to believe her. But why else didn't her mother tell her, or want her there? Was it only the box? Stef felt, somehow, that if she stayed longer, if she went upstairs, if she were alone with Uncle Jeff, she could find out.

Constance tried to stand in a more comfortable position; her back gave her trouble. "What if, Stefanie," her mother said—her tongue a deep red from her cherry Jubilee sour balls—"...what if she wanted to get you, too?"

Stef was relieved to have her hands in soap up to her elbows. She played with the water in the sink, looking forward to getting back to school, to rowing and the speed of the skull taking her away from all this. The Olsen dishes were full of chips and hairline cracks, so she slipped those into the trash, not wanting to handle them. The sun had gone down, and the remaining guests moved outside. From the kitchen window, she could see Tommy on her mother's lap, swaying back and forth. Stef was going to send him a present from the gift shop at school. She would have to really look to find the right thing. The Olsen boys were in the basement, blasting their music. She noticed her mother's ring left on the windowsill. Stef dried off her hands and slipped it on. It looked better on her, with her olive skin and long, thin fingers.

Carrying the dry dishes over to the pantry, Stef noticed a musty smell. Linoleum covered the floor, so it couldn't be the embedded odors of the old rug. She put her ear close to the door, careful not to touch the wood. She heard chattering. Feminine voices, kind of old and kind of young. When Stef opened the pantry, the voices got quiet, and the odor, like the smell of an antique dresser drawer, intensified.

Smiling, Stef imagined Grandma Dottie and Aunt Linnie on top of one another in the closet. Like conjoined twins. Arguing. Their heads shrunken, their bodies small and hidden in rags with no visible hands, sparse gray curls matted to their skulls. Hiding in the pantry as if they could fool her. Coming back to get her, Stef knew. It was the way they did things. It was their family legacy. Damned if it was going to be her. Damned if she was going to be the one with the swollen belly and the cancer look in her eyes. She left the kitchen, and, seeing her mother's purse, picked it up. The wrapped pearl inlay from Aunt Linnie's jewelry box fell out. She quickly picked it up, stuffed it back in, and looked for her mother, determined to put the purse in her hands, and, finally, to go home.

# VAPOR

# TOWARD THE NORWEGIAN SEA

It was Toshy's turn to get falling down drunk. Julian Asti gave her the pleasure tonight, and tomorrow night would be his turn. The falling down drunk could do anything he or she wanted to do to the other one that was sober—well, not sober exactly, just not falling down.

This was their fun while Toshy visited her new husband, Julian, for three days on her new passport, before fleeing back to St. Petersburg—to her studio apartment way behind the Alexandrinsky Theatre, to her ten-year-old daughter, Inga, and, God willing, with a little moo-la in her pocket and the smell of Julian Asti completely washed away.

"I have only three days to live—" Julian said, pulling her close, undoing her halter. Toshy was skinny and appeared bloodless. He could fit her whole breast in his mouth.

"Three whole days," she said. "A feast."

The triangular flaps of her halter fell down and she quickly took the strings and tied it up again.

"Not yet, buster," which sounded like "booster."

Julian's face was perspiring. He hadn't taken his Viagra yet, it seemed.

"This is your thyroid gland," he said, pulling back the elastic black choker from Toshy's throat, sucking a spot.

He was saying some shit about the function of the thyroid, and it was getting on her nerves. At first, she thought he was so smart. But if he was so smart, how come he had nothing now? From sheik to poor man.

Toshy pushed him away and lost her balance, noticing four unopened bottles of vodka on the counter. The sight made her feel generous toward him again.

She pulled him down gently onto the linoleum floor, thinking of the drink and where it would take her. She had the talent to leave her body and follow the images in her mind, letting her body perform on its own. For now she chose to stay with Julian, to bite him, but was afraid to let her teeth dig into his fatty shoulder. The thought of drawing blood, getting his blood into her mouth, well, she hated the taste. He slid his hand down her back and into her pants.

Toshy Vazov remembered the night, over a year ago, when she first met Julian Asti. She was dancing at Stella's on Forty-Third Street. There were no fog machines at Stella's, but other than that, the New York clubs were not that different than the ones at home. Except the place in St. Petersburg had a fancy bowling alley on the top floor, with dancers on platforms over the lanes.

That night her leg was around a pole, her head back, and the light above her coated her mouth with the taste of tinny fluorescence. A major bulb had blown out as she grinded the pole, causing the Americans to holler cherry jokes, the waft of liquor breath reaching her as she did her number in the dimmest light, sparks burning her skin here and there.

After the crowd calmed down, she did her usual act, one that was making a little name for herself. Her stomach was empty and taut. She closed her eyes, circling her pelvic muscles, then thrust her bottom up, and took off on the same flight she took every night:

In her mind she would see the rooftops of St. Petersburg, their onion shapes, their pointed spheres. She grinded the pole more aggressively, aware of one particular man in the front row. Was he an Arab? The dark circles under his eyes, the graying goatee. His fingers like Antonio Cleopatra cigars, he held his pinky high as if he were drinking out of a demitasse cup at the Kempinski Hotel.

She closed her eyes again and soared. She felt herself falling through the stage floor, bumping down through layers of earth, cold wind, and then air as hot as hell, until she fell through the gray Russian sky on the other side of the world from Stella's, landing on top of The Peter and Paul Fortress overlooking the dirty Neva.

Toshy and Julian were sitting on the kitchen floor.

"My turn," she said, getting up to fix two juice glasses of Smirnoff, one with ice for him. She lit a cigarette.

"I want every minute to count," he said.

She got down on his lap, sipped her own drink, then put both glasses on the floor. She held his head in her hands; it was twice the size of hers. His teeth were not good like other New Yorkers she saw on the trains. Julian left his wife for her, for this crummy place. He moved out of a brand new grand house in New Jersey, surprising his wife Amy with a farewell note. Apparently, she had no idea her husband was going to leave. How could she be so stupid? More stupid than herself? Toshy noticed a pile of unopened mail next to the front door, and later she would hunt out Amy's letters.

"What's she like?"

"Who?"

"Your wife, dumbo."

Julian took the cigarette from her and threw it up and behind him into the sink.

"Come to answer me, or I won't make you suffer."

"Just turned fifty."

"Wow. Drives a fancy car?" Toshy bounced on his lap, her hands on an imaginary steering wheel making a sharp turn.

"She's been cruising this neighborhood. Rings my door-bell, too," he laughed, stretching his thick neck toward the ceiling as if he could see out the front window from the floor.

"What does she do all day?"

"Could never figure that out."

"She goes to nail salon!"

"No. She's a nurse. In a pediatrician's office. Three days a week."

Toshy fed him another sip to keep him talking. "A nurse for kids?" She took his wrist and started to *tap, tap*. She pictured a brunette with bright red lipstick and heavy tits. But nothing like a nurse. She must be nice.

Julian kissed Toshy through bangs that were as blonde as she could make them. "This is your night," he said. He got up with a lot of effort; his knees could not support his weight from the American football in college.

He went into the bathroom, and Toshy heard the click of the lock. She was not allowed to lock the bathroom door when she went in. She usually left it open and chatted while she peed anyway.

"I'll be waiting," she said. "Time to start the suffer game!"

Toshy hoped that he had a new *equation* to use on her—not like the last *sensitivity analysis*, which drove her nuts. It was much easier to learn English words this way than on the cards.

She looked around to see what she could take, but there was nothing of value, not even a watch. He was taking so long she was getting bored.

A thumping noise came from the bathroom.

"Please," he called to her. "Tosh. I need help."

She hurried toward the door, suddenly excited for the game. But wasn't it she who was supposed to do the suffering tonight? Wasn't it her turn?

"So you want all the pain for yourself?" Toshy laughed, wiggling the door handle. This was going to be good. In the bathroom! God knows what the goon had in store for her. Maybe he still had some fun in him the way he was when he was rich.

"Hey! It's locked!"

"Wait," he garbled, and she heard him inch on the floor. His hand slapped at the doorknob until it clicked.

Toshy opened the door slowly. She had her eyes closed because she couldn't stand it. The door wouldn't budge on Julian's foot, so she squeezed in, daring herself to look. His skin was as gray as the tile he lay on. He looked like the creature found on the beach of the Azov Sea, with rotating eyeballs.

At first, she thought he was actually in trouble, but then she realized he was just playing. She immediately sat and bounced on his stomach, watching his eyes flutter; then, she started to smack his face, first one cheek then the other. But his belly felt cold and slimy. Maybe she was stupid, but she wasn't going to let him fool her.

"You lie here and suffer while I get a drink." She hummed the boom-boom tune she'd heard in the cab. She slid off him and went into the kitchen.

"Tosh. Please."

He even changed his voice.

She saw his prescriptions for his heart trouble lined up on the counter. The stupid ox probably didn't take them, afraid he wouldn't be able to do it to her if he took all the stuff. How true.

Toshy took a swig of the vodka. She could hear him yell for her and she was tired of him, tired of this game. Everything had to be his way. She bet his wife never played with him. Toshy took the photo of Julian and his wife she found in a pile and studied it. She was wearing a classy pants suit, her head tilted toward her husband. A very nice lady. Had to be, giving little kids shots, holding babies. She took the photo of Julian and his wife and turned it over. It was easy to write in Julian's plain old block letters he used on the English cards:

*I know you are thinking about killing me. But, I have suffered enough. I am very sorry I had to leave. Julian.*

Toshy put the photo in one of the envelopes there, addressed it to his New Jersey mansion, and would remember to drop it in a mailbox on the way to the airport.

She walked into Julian's bedroom with her glass. Here was another group of vodka bottles lined up as if her new chemist husband had filled them up with clear solutions. There just couldn't be so much for free! She was so unsteady now, the bottles blurred and swelled at the top. They began to bend from their mid sections like the New York Rockettes with the reindeer antlers tied to their heads. Ever since Julian took her on the best date she ever had to Radio City Music Hall, she visits the Rockettes on their website. All their moves have inspired her choreography. They prepared for performances by doing wall squats, a big rubber ball behind them, legs open. Toshy stole from the hardest workingwomen in show business and made the moves something all her own.

Now she was getting queasy, the smoked sprats weren't sitting well, but she wanted to be in tip-top shape, the winner. From the hall, all she saw was a wedge of the belly with graying patches of Julian's hair, the rim of his white Jockey briefs with the red and blue waist band. And, why did he have to wear *those* kind of undies that were made for little boys?

His hands were flat out at his sides, palms up. On a regular day his hands were controlled by the emotion he carried in his heart, for her, waving, clapping, pinching (the pinching she couldn't stand) using his fingers with the drama of Ulyana Lopatkina on that old poster plastered on the wall in the metro.

"Julian Asti!" she yelled from the doorway, just to be sure. For a moment, she wondered if she were pronouncing his last name correctly; perhaps that was why he was not responding. To teach her.

"Julian!"

He wasn't used to drinking so much vodka at once. She hoped he would sleep it off. Sometimes he did that after he had his way with her, but they hadn't done anything yet, that's for sure. She had such ideas for the game; she had planned it all in her head on her way from Kennedy, but nothing like this.

She slipped into the bathroom, made a towel roll that she put under his neck then closed the bathroom door.

Toshy went and pulled all of the wife's letters, holding them out like a fan. She could not decide which one to open. She decided on one that had a smudge of lipstick on the back where the wife must have licked. She smelled the envelope, but nothing.

Although English was not easy to read, hers had improved since she met Julian. He could have been a teacher with his patience and his little cards with words on them. He would test her and flip them over. If she was correct, a surprise was in store. He never forgot to tally her mistakes, because for those she had to pay exactly as he proposed.

She opened the letter.

*Dear Julian,*

Toshy put her finger on the perfect script, picturing the lady from the photo, sitting at a fancy desk in front of a window with a cup of Royal Tea:

*I had to hear about your woman from your mother. Of course, she had to say the usual hurtful things. She was so busy calling me inflexible that she lost sight of our twenty-two-year marriage, Robbie, and how I have doted on both of you. She said she was hardly surprised at the kind of woman you are with—an "analytical man such as yourself requires a high level of mental stimulation." If you really need a Russian scientist, temporarily, go ahead. You never had a mid-life crisis so I guess this is it. But it's time to end this and get back to our lives. I took our vows very seriously. In front of God. I will not allow you to throw me away and talk alchemy with Ms. Brilliance!*

*I need to speak with you. The insurance, our taxes. They are going to come after us. I can't even pay these utility bills! I tried your office and no one will give me any information. Do you know how many times I have driven over to that depressing place and rung the bell and you are never there? Why can't you at least call me? ~Amy*

The bills that must rack up in a house like that. How could he do this to his last wife? Toshy couldn't even picture this kind of Julian. She hoped that Amy would feel better when she gets Julian's apology on the back of the photo.

Toshy caught herself in the mirror. Her white bangs pushed forward, the rest of her rockin' hair sticking up in the back, the black rimmed reading glasses Julian bought her at CVS. All she needed was a little urine cup.

Yes, she had quite a large specimen to deal with. She had never thought about being a scientist before. In fact, she hated science more than any other subject in high school.

Toshy remembered her bio teacher, Babkin, the wise-cracker, who never got off her back. When the class had to make a slit in the paper-thin skin of the frog to remove the heart, Toshy couldn't do it. The smell of formaldehyde always made her puke. Babkin went home after class but made Toshy stay late to finish. Toshy asked Vadim to remove the heart and pin it down on the Styrofoam and she would label it. The boy loved doing that stuff anyway. Then she asked him to cut out all the rest, the lungs, liver, pancreas, gallbladder, testes and anus, and to wrap them in the paper towel and give them to her. He said it was a lot of fucking dog shit for her to ask of him. Toshy knew instinctively, without a plan or a recipe, that she would be making chewy cookies for Babkin. When Vadim was done dissecting, he put the empty skin sack left of the frog and put it on the tip of his finger, swinging it around saying it looked like a used condom and what was the big deal? Wasn't Toshy Vazov used to this kind of thing?

Toshy went into Julian's bedroom closet and put on one of his white office shirts. On her, it was a short dress. He used to wear these when he came into Stella's after the job at Chem-Tech Labs, with a jacket, tie, and those shoes that tied-up on the side for bad feet. She kept her Mary Janes with the wedge heel on.

Toshy went into the kitchen for a splash more. Everything was so quiet in the apartment, it was like walking in snow.

The box of Wonderful Bird Chocolate Souffles she had brought from Pulkovo International was still sitting on the counter. Beside the souffles, the flash cards were organized by Julian into mini towers. His Nu-salt was in the middle of the towers because he said he couldn't live without the taste. He said he longed for pink salt, the kind you grind. He would go on and on about salt like it was caviar. How the fake salt, Nu-salt, wasn't the same, and it was expensive. The first Julian could have bought lots of salt, no problem. She liked the kind at home that looked like rock candy.

Toshy opened the fridge and saw meat wrapped in white paper. This place was nothing but rich with finds. Even though she had no recipe, she was sure she could turn on the oven and cook the meat with lots of salt and it would taste just like the free samples of beef from the Kuznechny market. She took out the package and sat it on the counter.

The doorbell rang without quitting.

Toshy grabbed the pen and pad used for her English lessons and, with the focus of a scientist about to document her findings, went to answer the door.

Through the peephole, she saw a blonde woman. A gold cross around her neck. Toshy could take as long as she wanted to study her from behind the door! Such a pretty beige suit, and loafers made out of such a nice skin—was it rattlesnake? She looked just like the perfect woman in Julian's photos, except in person her pinkish-blue eyes were smaller than marbles. Her lips, thin and curling. She looked like she was inhaling and exhaling heavily. Toshy looked out to the sidewalk and saw a silver SUV in the shape of a huge bullet.

How could Julian walk out on this?

Toshy smoothed down her lab dress, held her pad at her waist, put the pencil behind her ear. In the back of her mind, somewhere, in that place where she never planned but just let things happen, she saw that she was about to make a new friend. She opened the front door, her heart knocking against her delicate breastbone. She shifted from one leg to the other, careful not to show off her shoes.

"Privetik!" she said.

The Amy woman stood there as if she was frozen in doomsday. "I'm looking for Julian Asti."

"Oh, ya, come in."

"Are you…?"

The woman stepped in, raising her feet higher than necessary, as if she were wearing astronaut space boots. She maneuvered around as though she didn't want to wake Julian, but she could not have known he was sleeping.

Toshy could see the tiny lines from the bottom of Amy's

74

simple nose to the top of her mouth, as if tiny strings were yanking on her lips. She walked into the kitchen with a look that might find Julian sitting at the table.

"Are you cleaning the house?" Amy asked Toshy. "In that getup?"

"No. I'm a scientist," Toshy said, holding up the pad.

"Oh my God. Where is my husband?"

"He's in the bathroom. Been in there a while. My husband, too," Toshy said softly in her own language realizing they shared the same misfortune.

"Then we all know what he's doing. Aren't these the good things in a relationship?" She walked around and came to the pile of letters. "Well, I see he opened one of them anyway."

Toshy was afraid to move from the spot she was standing. She wondered how she could get the chocolates to offer her guest.

"Who are you? *What* are you?" Amy asked in a tone too loud for the small apartment.

"I'm Natasha. I'm a scien—" Was Amy going to cry? "I'm so sorry," Toshy said, not sure what she was sorry for and moved over to reach for her hand even though touchy wasn't her thing.

"Can't wait to tell my know-it-all mother-in-law about your profession."

Amy tore away walking down the short hallway, opened a door that was a closet then slammed it shut. She found the bathroom. "Are you going to hide in your shit forever?" Amy yelled, banging away, her eyes shrinking.

Toshy stood behind her with the box of chocolates.

Amy turned around. "What the hell are you doing?"

Toshy held them out to her, but the woman did not take the offering.

Julian said Amy was *devout*. The wife believed in all that mumbo-jumbo. And, Toshy could bet her life that a string of candles somewhere burned for Julian. *I took my vows very seriously. In front of God.*

Toshy could not put her confession into English. It was too much, too fast. She started to tell the story of her and Julian in her own language. Amy would not know Russian, only Julian had learned the language, and it was only because he loved her so much. But someone like Amy, with all her feelings, would understand just by the rise and fall of her voice. The melody.

Julian had the papers from Chapel of the Bells stuffed somewhere around here in case Amy wanted to see them. He said he had to be the one to take care of the legalities, except for his own mail and bills apparently.

Toshy stepped closer.

"Get away from me, please," Amy said, her voice all techno and jumping octaves.

Still holding the tall box of chocolates in her hand like a chalice, Toshy began: Julian got the VIP table at Stella's and started to come every night. No matter what act she was performing, he was ringside—near the dance floor with the shower, in the chill-out room, observing her chain dance as if he were under hypnosis. (She brought her chain dance from the old club on the other side of the river from Nevsky Prospect but changed it for Stella's and the guys here named her "Slinky"). Then Julian took her out one Saturday night, and it was as if he made up his mind right then and there that he was going to marry her. It was fine with Toshy because she had to go back home soon to Inga, and she was broke.

On the first date Julian took her to the High Life for meat on the Upper East Side. She thought it would have been more elegant, but it was dark and disappointing. She couldn't see the carp in the tank with the film of green. He talked a lot about birds, especially the condor bird, one that he had been watching—or had been watching him—before he left his wife in New Jersey. These were the details of his life that he found so clever. Like he connected with birds in the sky. He ordered little glasses of scotch and asked her what she was thinking when doing her dance, the one she was known for, "Dirty Neva."

"Oh, no thinking. Never thinking. Dancing." Toshy let her head fall back on the leathery booth and she knew what *he* was thinking. His hand was under the table moving on her legs like a tarantula. She opened her legs and his finger inched in.

"Thinking now?" he said, picking up his drink with his free hand.

She imagined her insides, swelling like puff pastry around his dark skin. She did not look at Julian's broad face but pretended the finger inside her belonged to the pretty boy at the souvenir shop on Ostrovsky Square. She rocked in the booth.

"I make pictures," she said, waving her hand near her head.

The waitress came. "Here you go. Who gets black and blue?"

"That's yours, sure," Toshy said.

Toshy pushed out his hand and could not wait to taste her steak that would have not one bit of red in it.

As Julian wiped his hand on the napkin, watery red streaks veined out from underneath his t-bone and around the curly parsley while he was saying that it was impossible for the brain not to think. "In fact, that is what makes us human, that is what protects us in life. I think therefore, I am."

"Is that so?" Toshy said, gulping the vodka water because of all the ice they used in U.S.

"Where is wife right now?"

Julian looked around to the left, then the right. He told her the story quickly in a whisper, one-two-three.

"So make believe," she said laughing. New York men always told stories about leaving their wives.

"It's true, so help me God."

"Then why did big shot chemist stay, if he was so unhappy?"

"I stayed for our son."

"Oh, and he was lucky boy 'cause you stayed?"

"See, you do think."

"No, I don't booster. Thinking doesn't protect me."

Toshy dipped her steak fries in Julian's puddle of Worcestershire while he continued to talk about all the years with Amy.

Toshy closed her eyes and could see the McMansion with a glitzy chandelier hanging like an indoor planet when you walked in the front door. She saw the sloppy EZ chair where Julian sat in front of the TV. A hyper, silky-haired dog ran around in the backyard. She saw a garage with a nice cement floor as clean as a living room. She saw the dark-haired boy tearing out of the driveway in a fun car. And there was Julian, on his deck next to a grill that you turned on with a switch, staring at the condor bird hovering over him in the perfect sky.

That night after dinner, they went back to the apartment near Avenue A, which Toshy shared with some of the club's staff, and Julian was the one who wanted her to do weird things to him. "Experiments," he called them, to see how much he could endure. "I'm *in the field*," he announced as he sat on her bed with the flimsy spread that was nothing like what he was used to. He kind of rolled on the bed sweetly, a nice man having a nice time, as if he had been begrudged happiness his whole life but now had a smidgen of content-ment.

He put his thumbs under her eyes and said they both had the circles. Apparently, this bound them together somehow. He told her that the skin around the eyelids—*periorbital skin*—is the thinnest on the body. "When the blood passes through the large veins, the skin looks bluish."

"I'm Russian. I just look like a bird."

"A painted bird," he said.

Again, so clever.

Julian never said much about Amy after that night at the High Life, as if she were long dead. Toshy assumed that Julian's wife was just as miserable as he. That she wanted the divorce. She had no idea that Amy had no idea. How could Amy have no idea? Didn't she smell him when he came home?

Toshy told Amy in her own language, a sound which stopped and started like a noisy car, that she had been ad-vised by the Vegas wedding site to wear a rented dress with no sleeves because it was so hot there. The organs in her body might get burned through her *translucency,* and this is how she began to think hanging around with Julian Asti.

They honeymooned at Paris Las Vegas. The hotel gave them cookies and milk in the wedding package. "I mean are we kiddies?" she asked Amy as an aside in English.

But then Julian came to Russia for a visit—it took him forever to get cleared—and even there he acted like he knew everything, speaking the language, doing shots, teaching her about her own city! He knew everything there was to know about the cathedrals, the Fontanka River, the Griboedov Canal—and shouldn't they be doing chemical tests on the waters? Then he got sick in his heart. He had to fly back home for American care, and, every minute Toshy stayed in St. Petersburg without him, he said his heart got weaker.

"I don't want to hear your gibberish," Amy said.

"That is how we got married," Toshy managed to switch back to English quite easily.

"Married? That's impossible. He's already married. There are laws here."

"Well, I hope we didn't break the law," Toshy said with her stage face.

"Were you an abused child or something? Where in God's name did he find you?"

"I told you. Stella's. But I'm so glad to be back home, working at Fish Fatale. They have a beautiful crowd. You can dance over the tables. They have *levels.*"

This observation made Toshy stand more erect. She could bend her back any which way.

"You think I want to be with him now? Julian-the-Great?

That's what he called himself when he was walking around
St. Petersburg. Ordering cognac everywhere. And that sweating. He bought a mini of the Bronze Horseman. Look. It's
in his bedroom."

Amy came at her and Toshy braced herself for a slap. Amy
took the palm of her hand and pressed it on Toshy's mouth.
Just like Vadim and Georgy pressing their stinky palms so
hard she wondered if her teeth would go. Fat Georgy had
pinned her ankles down, then Vadim had done the same for
his friend. While Vadim poked her, he'd asked if she thought
his lab work was free of wages.

"I don't want to hear anymore and I don't want to even
touch you." Amy ran and put her hand under running water.
She shook them dry as she ran out.

Toshy followed. "You should be with him. I'm flying
home pronto."

Amy pushed the bathroom door in and saw Julian on the
floor. "Oh my God."

"No, he always sleeps like this. The drink is too much for
him and his pills and the Viagra. No good mix."

Amy was down on the floor next to Julian, her two fingers
pressing the inside of his heavy wrist. She put her mouth
on his and blew hard. She banged on his chest as if she was
trying to make a dent. Toshy wasn't sure when Amy took off
her blazer; she didn't remember seeing her do it.

Amy yelled something about 911, but she was already
dialing her cell phone with the elegant silver case.

The paramedics, the cops. Amy was still pounding.

Here they are, Toshy thought. *Polizmeisters* like the ones
that hung out in the lot behind the Fatale, pretending they

were there to arrest. And the big Sergei-type last week that wanted her bad, pleading for dildo dance off the menu. "I don't work the parking lot," she said and how perfect.

"She killed my husband! That little pig!"

"You are nothing like the picture!"

Toshy still had the box of chocolates in her hand. "I must go in there and see him." She walked in a performed trance, one that she had done many times.

She went into the bathroom, the floor too small for everyone on it and kneeled next to Julian. Amy was screaming for her to get out, for the cops to take her away.

Poor Julian wearing a death mask. Toshy smelled formaldehyde that rose off his body like a spirit. She felt the thick rise and twisting burn of the scraps in her stomach. The unstoppable vomit pushed out of her mouth and splattered on Julian's belly. The box of candy fell, and the Wonderful Bird Chocolate Souffles hit and rolled on top of Julian's privates.

The cops were soothing here in the U.S. and their peacefulness floated over to Toshy and put a sheath of calm around her. One took out an old-fashioned hankie from his pocket and gave it to Toshy to wipe her mouth.

"You okay there?" he asked, escorting her out of the bathroom. "How did this happen?"

"He was good man to me. A papa."

Toshy walked further into the living room. The cops followed her, and she knew they were checking her out. She felt a swing come on; her ass was like a little ball on a chain. "You know," Toshy said. "I wanted him to take the air of the Azov Sea. They say it cures you. He had affection in his heart."

She could hear Amy yelling the most disgusting things!

About her! Toshy would never be her friend now.

"Follow me," she said to the cops. "I ask you. Please."

She turned and went straight to the pile, and off to the side was the photo of Julian and Amy that she had planned on mailing on the way to the airport.

"I think he was afraid of her."

Toshy handed the cops the photo, turned it over, and showed them the note in Julian's block letters that began, *Dear Amy, I know you want to kill me...*

"Julian figured she might try a trick like this. She's a nurse and they know how to fool with meds. He gave her everything, then rented this dump for himself. He is a very smart man and comes from a beautiful home."

The boss of the two took the photo with Julian's letters on the back.

"He really suffered," Toshy said, her hand over her mouth with the smell of puke.

"Let's get at this," the other said.

"I have to go home to my Inga. I'm going to the airport, but I will be happy to help before I go."

As the cops walked to the bathroom, the paramedics were putting Julian's body on the gurney. With a cop on each side of Amy, they walked her out. Her feet were not even on the ground.

Toshy went into the kitchen and gathered up some things in a bag she pulled from the closet. There was so much vodka left! And the good meat! She was not a waster. She put a few bottles in the bag with the meat to cushion them, the noise of the others moved further away.

Alone, creating again in her mind, she could see a long

red chain hanging from the ceiling at the new club on the west side of the Fontanka Canal. More festive than Fatale. At this club they pretended it was a New Year's Eve every night of the week! She grabbed the chain and stood facing the audience in her T-back and furry pasties, giving them all a bird's-eye view. She had a noisemaker horn in her mouth. A sparkly top hat, the front tipped forward. Like Julian said the first time he saw her, she was as fair as the wings of a moth. And, they will all want her as much as he did.

What the buffoons in any audience didn't know was that the position of the head dictates the position of the rest of the body. Toshy could stretch one leg up the chain like a New York Rockette. She could attach her ankle to the links with her hand. Her other arm would do an over-head until she sank down to the floor and performed as if she were boneless. The Dirty Neva dance would be nothing compared to the number she was conjuring up now. And once she got back on stage at home, he would have the best seat—looming over her from grey skies, observing the exotic with Julian Asti intensity.

The men in uniforms were still out on the sidewalk with Amy. The strip of houses led down to a donut shop and a car place. Her apartment was poor too, but at least there she lived under the spell of the Alexandrinsky Theatre. She remembered walking to her apartment with Julian during his visit and how he said he felt the thumps from the orchestra in his chest. Now she realized it was just his affection because she hadn't felt anything in her heart that night.

Fixing her hair with a splash of water, Toshy was busy envisioning the Alexandrinsky dancers with their caps of soft black feathers tight on their heads, telling a violent story with their limbs. The mood of the ballet would rise from the Theatre's chimneys and fall on her like a sticky layer of dust.

Choreography was personal. Packing up to leave she became excited for the long flight where she would have hours to discover the soul of her composition. She loved looking over the wings of the plane, with the endless depth of the Arctic below, then finally to the Norwegian Sea, the energy of the waters shooting through her legs. No one could reach her in the air of her imagination. She wondered what name the men would give her this time. Flamingo? Loon? Little Sandpiper? Julian was right. The mind could never stop thinking.

# SOUNDS SKIMMING OVER THE ATLANTIC

Max took out his gigantic linen handkerchief and used it to remove a pepper from his breast pocket. He cracked open the red skin with the tip of his steak knife and sprinkled the seeds over his spaghetti. As he tossed, he explained to me in a secretive voice that touching the skin for even a second could burn your fingers. He wrapped the skin in the napkin so none of it was exposed and placed it in the ashtray.

The tables were dressed in checkered tablecloths, and Ruffino bottles substituted as candleholders.

"I haven't been in a place like this since I was a little girl," I said.

"Kath, you're still a little girl."

I was starting to miss my friends. *Top Cat's taking over*, they said of Max. They had a name for everybody and had started right in the day I met Max in the Prego Prego near NYU on Tenth, as we huddled over mozzarella sticks and a pitcher of beer. He had the kind of looks you'd find in an Italian movie with subtitles—dark messy hair in a ponytail half-in, half out of his shirt collar; blue, blue eyes; and a body so taut, it appeared as if a flesh-colored fabric had been stretched and fitted over his small frame.

Max owned a string of Prego Prego's, so when we had the chance, we tried different kinds of Italian. There, at

Carmella's, they tossed the pasta in a sauté pan right at your table.

He held up the garlic knots, tempting me.

"Max, I'll reek later."

"I'll suffer," he said.

Afterwards, in the car, between the heavy red wine and garlic, I was the one suffering. On the way to the party, I felt like I had to vomit as we drove down Montauk Highway. We had the top down, and I pressed my head on the back of the seat to keep it in place. Stars that should have been still and bright in the black Montauk sky were darting around as though they were looking for a better spot to hang, bumping others out of the way. I focused on the streamers they left behind like disintegrating tails. The shooting stars, along with the smell of salt and fish from the Atlantic, made me more dizzy and nauseous. I took an Izod shirt from under the seat and held it over my mouth.

Max pulled the car over, expertly hiding it in the brush and reeds at the entrance to a hidden driveway. He helped me out and stood behind me for support. With one hand on my stomach, the other hand on my forehead, he let me barf. He wanted me to. "There you go baby, come on…let it come up, don't fight it…come on…that's it…you'll feel like a million bucks again."

It was hard for me to imagine that a man like this, a man who took such care of me, hardly knew the affection of a mother. He had been so young when she died, he said his memories of her came to him very seldom.

"Tell me, about her. Please."

Max dampened his handkerchief with a fresh bottle of Evian and patted my face, the back of my neck. He looked as if he hadn't heard me, but I knew he was pretending.

As we drove to the party I didn't have the strength to speak. I watched Max and tried to picture him as a baby, alone in a big-wheeled carriage with no mother behind him. All I could see was the same forty-six-year-old jaw, with just the right amount of stubble I loved, jutting out of a lacy bonnet—an olive-skinned baby-man with a large bow tied under his chin.

Unlike Max, who had so little to hold on to, I could remember my own mother and had told Max, countless times, how she had been photographed again and again. One of our last moments together: I stood in the doorway and I could hear the thighs of the nurses, hissing, their heavy legs coated in thick nylon, rubbing together as they sashayed around the room, helping themselves to chocolates my mother would never eat again. They hoisted Mom up by her limp shoulders, making her chest a clear shot for the X-ray machine. And now I heard their sugary voices perfectly: *Lovely, you look so lovely today, Didi. We've come to take your picture. Did your daughter fix you up like that?*

I wasn't a talker and had stepped outside the door, standing in the hallway with a tube of lipstick and a comb in my pocket. I knew how much Mom did not want to be there, and I thought about how often I had stood in the hallway on the sixth floor at Sloan-Kettering, staring down at the waxy tiles, thinking I could see Mom's face in the reflection, looking up, begging me to get her out.

I have thought of this every day since she died. I'm not

sure why. I was only fourteen then. Max and I knew this motherless thing like no one else. And he never tired of my memory. I described it to him over and over again, and, in each version, I focused on something different—the way I applied Mom's Misty Mauve lipstick and blush, or the little tail on the comb that I used to make a French twist before they took the X-ray, even though she was in a coma.

I still carry one of those teasing combs and love making Max sit between my legs, my boobs against his back, fooling with his pony tail, or making a bun—guy types, of course. I tease him until he is absolutely dying. For me. In our sleepy moments, I tell him more stories, without demonstrations. He pulls my legs closer to him—they're longer than his, the top of my thighs (almost) reach his waist—and listens. Listens and measures.

By the time we reached the party on Dune Road I felt better, and Max was doing his thing to me. Talking to me with his car. He used his car as if it were his own body—slowly backing it up, moving forward, revving the engine, slightly going back and forth, first a little then a lot. But now he was saying something else. He was going so slowly into the driveway of my friends' rental, he didn't kick up any gravel, not one pebble. We rolled like miniature people in a child's play mobile, showing me he was uninterested in the whole party thing. Extravagant blue lighting, with rhythm, flashed over the roof, a perfect imitation of fireworks. Drew Richards, who wanted to be a lighting man, was up on a ladder at the side of the house. He was in the film department. I was in NYU's graduate program for Early Childhood Learning. Everyone else was getting their MBA's. You could always find

Drew up on a ladder, with wires round his neck like so many Hawaiian leis and a beer bottle in his back pocket, although he never took time out from his projects for a sip.

Max bypassed him as if he were a bird on a tree.

The house looked even saltier than last year's, with rotted buoys hanging off the gutters, the kind of place you couldn't damage, even if you tried. Every Fourth we ended up clearing one bedroom of beer cans, and all of us sacked out together.

Max pulled me around to the other side of the house, to a path that led down to the beach. He had his hand on my back, steering me.

"Just for a minute," I said, knowing Robin must be worried we were going to do a 'no show' again.

He pointed to a rusted anchor jutting out of the sand. "Watch out."

The back deck was high off the beach, loaded and sagging, and I wondered if it might collapse with everyone on it. I tried to scope out my friends, but I was quickly maneuvered toward the shoreline.

Max walked backwards facing me. "I'll never buy here— I'm trying to get away from New Yorkers."

"Who cares." I loved Max's sparse apartment, so close to the Central Park Zoo that we could look down and see the polar bears sloshing around in the phony Arctic.

"Shall we?" He offered me his hand.

We could see the rental from the beach, glowing on stilts, propped up like an old ship on the sand, but far enough away for us to be completely alone. I felt like I was spying on my own friends.

I sat down close to the water and Max lay down next to

me, leaning on one elbow. Most of his hair had fallen out of his ponytail. He put his foot on top of mine and scraped off the wet sand—"Breaded flounder-foot, ready for the fryer."

I was thinking of sharks tooling around out there, and how there is nothing beautiful about the ocean at night.

"Come on, lie back." He unzipped my pants discreetly, even though no one was around, and pulled up my t-shirt just a bit. "Here?"

"No, down further."

"Here?"

"No, down further and to the right."

He kissed my stomach, near the hipbone. "Here."

"Yes." I put my hand over his mouth: "That's exactly where I gave her the shots."

"Nurse Kathy."

"Oh Max, you know the raw pizza dough that sits in the silver bowls in Prego? That's exactly what her skin was like. I had to squeeze a roll of it." I tried to pull my skin from my stomach to demonstrate, but it didn't even come close. "So she'd feel a blunt jab. Not a sharp one."

"At night?" Max asked, but he already knew the answer.

"Two shots in the morning and two at night. Do you believe that? We used to say, 'Just our luck.'"

"Tough old broad."

"She wasn't a broad, Max, she wasn't even old."

"Sorry. You knew how to do the syringe? At that age?"

"They were pre-measured injections—it was like taking a straw out of its paper wrapper. Looked like yellow perfume."

"How long did that go on?"

"About six months. Until she went back into the hospital."

"And, where was your dad?"

"Working, mostly."

We must have gone through the story twenty times before, but now I added the perfume part. The gold liquid. Max slipped his hand inside my jeans.

"I think I know what it's like to have a baby, Max. I mean—I know what it's like to take care of one."

"Me, too."

I could faintly hear Handel's *Water Music* now rousing me out of a gooey, familiar place. Every Fourth, I was tricked into thinking these soft horns and pipes were natural sounds skimming over the ocean toward us on the deck of our annual rental—but Drew piped it in for his lighting show. It all worked together with the fireworks that were shot off by a private club further up the beach, where the nice houses began.

I got to my feet, zipping and brushing myself off, and started back toward the house. Max came up behind me, the bottoms of his white pants rolled up. I reached for a comb in his back pocket and was surprised to find Mom's old comb with the pointy tip.

"Leave your hair the way it is," he said, stepping away from me.

"I want to go in through the front," I said. "It would be like we just arrived."

We were silent, walking through the sand, as if we were carrying something heavy between us. The spray off the water hit my face in sharp pings. We snuck between two other houses to get to the front so that we wouldn't be seen from the deck.

In the humid living room, bodies moved as if floating through a thick solution. When Robin kissed me on the cheek I felt her damp face. She shook Max's hand, flashing her diamond.

"The bathroom floor is soggy," she said. "Hope you don't have to go." She glanced at Max's leather sandals. I noticed a drop of vomit on one of them.

Robin began digging Max for info. She started in with possible entrees for her wedding, and as I left to search for the others, she was already onto, "So, Max, were your parents in the restaurant business?"

Eddie had worn his sneakers heels out, so the backs of his shoes were mashed down. "Top Cat let you out?" he said, yanking on the belt that hung off my waist. A new purple-headed girlfriend in a tube top was at his side. Robin's fiancé was there, too, already acting like a husband, avoiding Robin.

"He's right over there and coming this way," the girlfriend added.

"Of course he is," Eddie said, putting his finger through the loop of my earring pretending it weighed a ton.

Robin arrived with Max, her arm around him. She was twice his width. Max was studying Eddie, his finger still in my earring. Max let go, did his handshake all around. When he got to Eddie, they shook hands slowly. His hair was neatly slicked back into his ponytail again.

He was trying, but I wondered if he could ever be one of us. I had hoped I could introduce him to my father, but when I'd told Dad I was involved, he'd said, "What kind of individual calls himself Max?"

Max pulled out a vial and threw it to Eddie.

"Good man," Eddie said, with only a touch of thanks, and immediately put it into the pocket of his cargo shorts.

I was a little taken aback by this because me and my friends really weren't into coke—neither was Eddie, not much—and all Max did was drink a little red wine or beer.

Max put his hand on my back and pressed me close to him. "Educate your friends. Teach them a real buzz."

And then, in front of everyone, Max took my face, held it with both hands, and kissed me on the mouth as if we were completely alone. I was into the show and would have taken this as far as he wanted to go until I tried to move away and felt his hands tighten around my face like a clamp. I put my hands deep in his front pockets and discreetly pressed my fingers into him, until he got the message to stop.

Max pulled me through the crowd. I looked over my shoulder and saw Eddie, Robin, her fiancé, and now Drew, watching.

The place was packed and I wondered if all these people would be at Robin's wedding. A girl in gym shorts, a bikini top, and sun-burned chest, didn't move out of Max's way. She was so wasted she probably never saw me towering behind. He put his hands on her hips, she put her arms around his neck, her bottom lip practically dangling. They stood there, staring, until he gently moved her to the side.

We finally made it out to the deck where I could breathe. I concentrated on the sound of waves under the *Water Music*, Drew's lighting flashing around us like a heartbeat on its way out. Guys with their collars turned up and Vuarnets on royal blue strings around their necks, leaned against the railing, holding cups of beer. I felt them looking, but I wasn't sure if they were interested in me, or Max and me. I was almost a head taller and downright pale in comparison, not to mention the age thing. However, no one ever mistook him for my father.

"I see we're big on the Country Day crowd here—getting bankrolled by mom and dad," he said in the lowest of Max voices as he pressed the lever on the keg. He reminded me how he had caddied for these types as a teenager to support himself. I guess that's how he learned to dress—clean and pressed Polo shirts, deck shoes—because he wasn't the preppy type. He talked to a couple of the guys, shifting his beer from one hand to the other in constant motion.

By that time the fireworks display had started, and everyone was coming out to the deck. I worried it would collapse. Robin headed toward me, the smell of rum rising in a vapor from her plastic cup.

Robin had a thing about Drew, like she was his mother. "I know he's waiting for his chance with you. To have a real relationship. Why can't you go for *normal?*"

I pointed out that Drew was doing pretty well for himself—under a strobe in the corner of the deck, practically sucking the face off a tan girl with a bleached pixie haircut.

"Look, Kath." Robin was all tanked up, swinging her cup in sync with the rise and fall of her worries, the concoction flying out and dripping down her arm. "Max is like too closed up or something. And he's always got one eye on you."

"You don't get it."

"Don't get what?"

"Things happen with Max."

Eddie's girlfriend came over, the only heels on the deck, and demanded to know who we were talking about.

"Max," Robin said, downing her cup. "Mr. Obsession."

"He's packed."

I saw Max coming toward us, with a shine on his forehead, managing four cups of beer. Several napkins were stuffed in his hip pocket, and I wondered where he had found them.

Robin and Eddie's girlfriend couldn't take their eyes off him. He was nothing like Eddie, or Drew or Robin's fiancé. And, while he was charming them, he was doing it all for me, watching me with a vigilance that said, *Whatever you want baby.* But it wasn't just that—and that was intoxicating in and of itself—it was the thing I could never put my finger on. Max was a mysterious mix. He never wanted you to do anything for him; he wanted to please you, wanted you to be yourself. So there you were, all happy and unaware, in the heart of his secret plan, until he slipped his two slim fingers inside you and helped himself to your soul.

The beer was warmish and I couldn't get it down. I was still a little queasy. None of us said much while the skyrockets took off, straight into red and blue bursts, exploding into invisible walls. Robin had her head on my shoulder—I was just the right height for her to lean on when she got like this.

"Let's catch the rest of it down there, in our spot," Max said to me and Robin.

"I'd rather not." It seemed like too much of a trip. "And besides," I whispered over Robin's head. "She's in no condition."

He put his arm around her and carefully led her to a chair. "Just till the show's over. Come on," he said. "Then we'll come back and take your college friends out for some real food."

We walked down the wobbly staircase to the beach. Max left his sandals by the wall. Drew and the pixie girl had moved down onto the sand. Iridescent greens like an immense bowl of sequins spilled above us. As we got farther from the house, the party noise was replaced by the sound of the ocean.

Max had that familiar look on his face that said 'alone at last.' I could tell he was gearing up for one of my stories, circling my lower back with the palm of his hand as we walked, but I just wasn't up for it. When it came to memories, I was the sole giver—I scraped up everything in me and never got one tidbit in return.

"You never told me one story about your mother, Max, you know that? Not one."

"That's because I've only got one and I've been saving it. When you're ready, of course."

"Make it worth my while." I had a vision of Robin passed out on the deck and people stepping over her.

"You sure you want to hear it? It's not much, but it's my one and only."

"Bring her to me."

Max turned away and faced the Atlantic, as if he preferred it to me. Perhaps the expanse of water led to a door, and he wasn't sure what was on the other side. He stood there, unaware of my presence. It was the only time I remembered being forgotten by Max, and it was an eerie feeling.

He was already talking, and I was afraid I had missed something.

"I remember her head hanging over the sink. I could see her eyes upside down, and she was talking to me as she did it to herself. I was on the edge of the bathtub."

"Did what?" I interrupted him and took his hands. He had to let go of me and stare out at the ocean before he could continue.

"She worked with a plastic bottle full of a thick, dark purple solution, and she was sticking the spout in her hair, hard, rubbing it in rows, back to front, front to back, and the slimy shit stank like a skunk—she used to say that—all mashed in the roots of her hair, and she kept going until her scalp was completely covered. 'Max, hand me the powder. Get me the towel. Max, stamp out the cigarette, will ya? Max, get lost.' I could never figure out what she was doing, in her black underwear and bra with her tits spilling out, her head upside down in the pint-sized sink."

"I know, Max." I tried to kiss him on the cheek. "It was just peroxide."

"Yeah, I know. She was a blonde, all right. Hotter than hot. 'Touch me and you'll burn like hell.' She said that, too." He was laughing at this point. "And, that's it. That's all I've got. That's all I remember about my mother—her squinty eyes, upside down, the butt from her Pall Mall burning in the top of a bottle cap. Oh yeah, the most memorable, Kath, I can still see them. The white plastic gloves she wore that made her hands look dead."

He shut his book. I knew I'd never hear it again. This one story, the only story, was mine now, too.

At least now I could finally see Max as a toddler, with shiny black hair, on the edge of a bathtub with a Matchbox car in his hand, watching his mother.

"I think this is exactly where we were before," he said as he stood there.

I started to get down on the sand, and he stopped me.

"Wait." He took his large handkerchief out of his pocket. I began to realize how much like a magician he was, something stuffed in each pocket for the most opportune times. He yanked it through the air, waving it around, draping it into a perfect square and laid it on the sand. "For you."

I sat on it, pretending to be an old-fashioned lady with a gentleman who has just laid his coat over the mud so she could enjoy the royal fireworks.

We were under the grand finale now. Cannons were being shot off out of order like a pirate ship not too far out in the distance. Handel's "Overture" had been cranked up from wherever Drew did that sort of thing. Reds and blues were dripping so low in the sky that I imagined warm sulphur washing over us, getting into our mouths.

Max made me lift my butt, and I thought he was going to put his hand under me, but he swiped the handkerchief, stealing back his prop.

The fireworks display was over. There was no difference between the horizon and what was above or below it. White foamy edges of the waves inched closer. Max took the handkerchief and started to wrap my head, turban style, the kind people wear after they've had brain surgery.

"Oh, no, please Max, not this. Let's go back," I said.

He continued carefully making a roll around my head, as if he hadn't heard me. He studied me, his hands on each side of my head.

I traced his eyebrows with my fingers. Thin arches that looked drawn on with charcoal pencil on a man I guess I didn't know after all.

"So," he said, in the gentlest of Max voices, "Tell me again, about the last surgery, after it spread to the brain and you…"

"Let me lie down." I don't know why I wanted to lie down, maybe from a certain kind of exhaustion. Max adjusted the turban so it was low on my forehead. I closed my eyes and saw Mom, who was saying no to what Max was doing, like it was hurting her, too.

"Max, I can't. I can't do this. Please." I rolled over to my side and felt Max's hands pulling me over on my back again, looking for that spot, his fingers searching my stomach. I brushed his hands away.

I slipped off the turban and got up. Max was jacked up on his elbow. He began writing in the sand with a broken shell.

I walked along the water's edge toward the house. The moonlight made a zigzag path that shimmered on the surface of the ocean. The icy water numbed my feet, and my bones felt as though they were going to crack. I kept walking, relieved I had never told Max about my very last moment with Mom. I'd saved that one. The bubbly raspy sound. The water in Mom's lungs that drowned her. The pressure that passed right through me.

I was afraid to look back, so sure that Max was walking behind me. But when I got further away, and finally turned to look, Max was still where I'd left him, lying on the sand, flat on his back, throwing his large white handkerchief in the air and letting it float down, until it fell neatly over his face.

# NOT THAT KIND OF VIEW

Gray and Shauna Pope stood outside their old apartment door, wiggling their key in the lock, trying to get it open just the way they used to. "Here, let me," Gray said, gently nudging his wife to the side. "I've got the touch." *Click*. He pushed the door open and heard the familiar squeak in the hinges, which sounded like *hee-haw-hee*. They hadn't been there in six months, since before the baby was born. Shauna's father left the apartment to her in his will. They used to live there full-time; now it was a vacation spot.

"Gray—everything's the exact same." Shauna walked into the stuffiness and stood in front of the six-foot oil painting, her hands at her sides in a little girl stance. The painting hung on a wall you could see from the hallway. It was a painting of a man, standing, with a bird in his palm, and a fish out of water at his feet. His shorts poofed out in the thigh. He wore maroon stockings, velvet shoes that curled up in the toe, and his hair in a pageboy cut. "There he is, Gray. Our Monk Man hasn't changed one bit." Satisfied, Shauna headed into the kitchen.

"He's not a monk—but tell him to shut his reverent eyes in about fifteen minutes," Gray said, snooping around, breathing in the old excitement. "He's the medieval type—bathed once a month. Probably liked his women that way, too," he added to himself.

"He *is* a monk. He just shed his robe. No more twelve rules to live by. He's got his own rules."

101

"I don't want to hear his rules right now." Gray was used to this—his wife, her fictional add-ons. An odd strain ran in her family. He was finally learning to shrug it off.

The first thing Gray did was stand in the bedroom doorway and check out the familiar space under the bed, partially covered by a shag rug, the one he'd carried up twenty-one flights in a roll that had felt as heavy as his future. They had one of those high, country beds, the kind you need a little two-step to get up on—even though it really didn't fit in size or style in their bedroom. Shauna had wanted a completely new look so she wouldn't be reminded of the way it had been when her father had lived here.

Gray took the dust mop from the supply closet and pushed it under the bed, near the woodwork and around the rug. "Yep," he yelled out to his wife, giving the mop a shake. "Everything is A-OK."

Gray walked into the bathroom and started running the water in the sink and bathtub at full force, until it went from watery brown to pure, Grade A, New York City water. The best. He flushed the rusty bowl once to fill it with water, and then flushed one, two, three times, until the water flowed anxious and responsive once again.

"Oh my God, Gray, why now!" Shauna yelled from the kitchen.

It was funny how without their baby, Audra, around, Shauna turned into her old baby self, with that munchkin voice, the one that needed Gray for *everything*. He found Shauna in the kitchen. A smell was coming from the refrigerator, but why did Gray have to deal with that now?

"Please, Gray, we can't have this smell while we're here.

You know," she said, looking down at herself as if she was envisioning their time alone later. "Please," she said, clipping her nose with her fingers. Bravely, she looked for the offender.

Shauna *was* brave, about so many unfortunate circumstances in her fortunate life—the suicide of her muckity -muck father, a drunk mother who had increasingly lost interest in her, an older brother who had cut himself off from her after their father's death. Although to look at Shauna, you'd never suspect she'd been cheated out of the basics. Her facial expression was always hopeful.

The perpetrator in the fridge was obviously the green, lumpy, previously orange block of cheese. It was the only type of cheese Shauna ever cooked with—American. Gray got the industrial garbage bag from the hall closet, swaddled his hands in dishtowels, removed the cheese, threw it into the bag, and quickly secured it with extra-long twist-ties. He ran the bag out the front door, holding it out in front of him, directly to the garbage room down the hall. (One of the old ladies must have been cooking bacon.) This was something he would have enjoyed as a kid. He saw himself playing an FBI agent, black windbreaker billowing out a bit as he ran down the hall of an Upper East Side apartment building, wearing a serious, putrid-cheese expression on his face. Trim and medium, he was light on his feet, but, he admitted, a little too good-looking for undercover.

When Gray returned, the kitchen window was open, and Shauna, now in Playtex gloves, was spraying Lysol. He jogged around the apartment, a few steps backward and a few steps forward, checking behind things, pulling books off the shelf and letting them fall on the floor—still in agent form—and called out to his wife, "Found it!" His hand fingered the bag behind all those issues of *Business Week*, where Shauna's father had been listed "Best CEO of the Year" for several years, the gold bookmarks sticking out of the tops. The articles highlighted his philanthropic generosity, accompanied by photos of him with inner-city children and board members of the older New York charities. As Gray's fingers walked over the magazines, he tapped his father-in-law's photos and thought, *Hey, asshole, you had everything to live for.*

Gray waved the sandwich-sized Ziploc—not even a quarter-filled with pot, about two joints' worth. He stuck his nose in the bag and sniffed for freshness. "We'll make do," he said. He knocked the six-month-old magazines off the cocktail table while Shauna dipped her sponge in a bucket of Mr. Clean.

The moment Shauna infused the kitchen with a mountainy fresh smell, Gray made a decision that would affect them for the rest of their married lives. He decided this is what they would use this place for—to keep themselves intact. The kid (he realized Audra was too young to call a kid, but pretty soon she'd have that long, wavy hair, and drift around him the way her mother did) would never see the inside of this place.

Gray picked up a *Parents Magazine*, opened to a random page, and dumped the pot onto a picture of a blue-eyed, cue-balled, double-chinned infant. He was surprised they even had this magazine, but the mailing label said Lenox Hill Hospital, where Shauna had worked before Audra was born. He sifted out the seeds and let them fall in the seam of the magazine; he covered the baby's drool with the usable leaves as he tilted it up next to the article, "Is Too Much Fantasy a No-No?"

He sat on the leather couch—the place had a completely different look from their new, old house in Larchmont with the wrap-around porch—and let the view do to him what it always did. He was relieved about so many things today; one, he had his wife all to himself, without Audra sucking on her every minute; two, it was simply a day off from the trade floor. Shauna was always afraid being a trader downtown would turn him dirty and volatile. He had almost turned dirty when his boss's girlfriend came on to him the other night—it would have been easy. And, volatile—well, he had his moments.

They couldn't see the water that encircled Manhattan from their living room window—it wasn't that kind of place—but the surrounding apartment buildings made a strong jagged fortress, their windows were a switchboard pattern of yellow against the black night. While Shauna fawned over the Monk Man, Gray had this painting—his blinked with life. He never felt mentally claustrophobic here the way he did in the suburbs, shying away from guys his age that, he felt, were parochial, playing poker in the basements of golf clubs. Their cigars—not one Cohiba among them—were emblems of what they thought was style. Here, the buildings were a beautiful distance from Gray and Shauna's apartment—there seemed to be fields and fields of open space outside the windows of the twenty-first floor, a long fluent ride to the next co-op, according to his mind's rail system.

Gray could point their standing astral telescope into any one of those windows and dip into a kitchen or a bedroom. The windows in the stairwells were good tidbits also. He wasn't looking for sex, not really. It was like flipping through every satellite channel, only the sound was on mute: a Confederate Flag substituting as a curtain (that was his center marker); the roommates who were re-building the Twin Towers out of beer cans on the table in their kitchenette; the woman with the balcony who never slept—and he would be back to check on her that night. Once, when skimming, he believed he saw two priests.

While he finished rolling, Shauna stood very still by the kitchen window, in one of her trances. She had dewy ethereal looks, as if she walked on a vapor fresh from a myth. She must have been thinking of her father, and Gray didn't intrude. In one of Shauna's rare, open moments, she had told him that as a little girl she used to sit by her father's bed when he was unable to get up—during his on-again-off-again depression—hold his hand, sneak a puff of his cigarette, and tell him Monk Man stories. Sometimes, she would hide under his bed and stay there until he fell asleep.

How many years ago did all that happen? Gray was beginning to wonder if Shauna was hiding something. The way he saw it, the poor Irish bastard had been sick—while his wife had been in the kitchen, he'd walked down the hallway from this very same apartment, up the stairwell and onto the flat roof. Gray found himself imagining the scene, the focused and humble look he must have had on his face, much like Shauna's. When they moved in after the wedding, Gray scraped the paint off every wall, hoping to get rid of any residue of mental instability his father-in-law may have left in the air.

Gray watched his wife from where he sat in the living room. He missed that close proximity in their house. The longest strands of her hair in the back reached the pockets of her jeans. The first time he'd met her at a party in a loft downtown, she'd reminded him of a woman with a flower crown, hiding in a mossy glen. The see-through skin. He'd had to lure her out of the woods and into a conversation. Now, Gray wondered if she was simply having baby withdrawals. If so, he was doomed.

He was admiring his work, holding up two even joints so his wife could see. Not the freshest, but the smell would destroy any trace of cheese. She didn't seem to notice.

"Hello, hello, are you there?" Gray asked. Granted, his wife was a head-in-the-clouds type—an English lit major—but there was plenty going on. He just couldn't figure it out. Shauna claimed she couldn't understand him, especially when he partied all night with his friends, sometimes over at the bar in The St. Regis, and didn't call to say he was in no condition.

"Oh, Gray, I don't believe it," she said, looking out the window. "He's still here."

Gray knew exactly whom his wife was talking about. The arm, the hand, the cigarette, whatever. Shauna called him The Smoker. Their other neighbors on the floor were old women who never seemed to die off, probably because of rent control.

"His wife can't take it," she said. "The wife is an ex-smoker, and the smell is intoxicating to her. But he doesn't have the willpower to quit, of course. He is actually pretty thoughtful. He hangs his hand out the window, so as not to tempt her. Later, she smells his fingers."

Gray knew his wife smoked an occasional cigarette on the

sly. He also knew she would attach a story to the arm. "Oh, did you decide he's married? Fuckin' weirdo probably lives alone. Maybe all the guy needs is a night out with the boys." Gray was good at providing temporary solutions.

"He's not so weird. Do you see the way he dresses? Perfectly starched white shirts, rolled neatly and evenly to the elbow."

"The way his *arm* dresses?"

"He has some wardrobe, I can tell."

Shauna stood at the window watching the cigarette between two thick fingers; the smoke rose and coiled in a noose. She appeared mesmerized as if she were watching a genie's bottle. "See—not between the tips, but between the fingers near the knuckles. Macho type. And, look at that watch."

"A match. I need a match." Gray was digging around. "Guess I could yell over to that fucker," he muttered.

"You know what, Gray? He's going to smell our stash after we light it," Shauna said, her Playtexed hand on her hip. "Our smoke is going to go out our kitchen window and directly into his living room and up his nose."

"Believe me, the cheese will get him first." Gray looked under the couch. "Maybe we don't like that shit coming over into our window. Second-hand smoke and all that. If you know where his apartment is, we should get the cheese out of the garbage and put it outside his door. A little something for our neighbor."

"I do know. 21X."

"There are no X's."

"I don't know why I even bother to talk to you, Gray. You never believe a thing I say."

"Let's take a walk down the hall—for proof. I want all of this over in about three minutes, so we can start doing what we came here to do."

The phone rang.

"Shit," said Gray. "Don't answer. Has to be a telemarketer anyway."

"You know damn well who it is. Mrs. McCarthy."

"You gave her this number?" They had left their cell phones at home in compliance with the vacation weekend rule.

"What's wrong with you?"

"The old bag knows the origin of every fart, burp, and ounce of spit-up. That's what she's calling about now. She gets off on that shit—makes her life meaningful."

"Hello, hi." Shauna peeled off her plastic glove with her teeth. Gray could see her thinking in a bubble over her head: *Maybe Audra was lying on her back—to prevent SIDS—but choked on her spit-up.*

Mrs. McCarthy wanted to know where the rectal thermometer was, in case she needed it during the night. She always did a run-down of supplies.

Gray lit the joint.

Gray and Shauna were high and dry-mouthed, and went under the bed to their old spot. There must have been two-and-a-half feet under there, plenty of room to flap against each other like two fish caught in a net. Gray was used to Shauna's milky scent now. It was as if her skin had just started to turn from nursing so her smell was a little off. Gray's face was mashed between his wife's legs when the phone rang again.

"The phooone—oh my God, the phone, Gray. Oh, God, something happened to Audra. I knew it. I knew this would happen. This is what we get for being selfish."

Shauna turned herself over, practically twisting Gray's neck, until she shimmied on her stomach and elbows out from under the bed and onto the parquet floors. "I can't deal with another surprise," she said on all fours.

Gray wanted to believe that Shauna was still under the bed with him, so he sent Shauna Number Two out to answer the phone. Gray and Shauna watched Shauna Two get to her feet and run out of the room in lanky strides. Gray thanked the original Shauna for not being so fucking responsible like Number Two, for putting him first in her life the way she should, for her devotion, and he began to kiss her.

The phone rang and rang.

Gray heard panic in his wife's voice.

"Mrs. McCarthy? Mrs. McCarthy? Hello, hello, is Audra OK?"

*If you would like to make a phone call, please hang up and dial again. Use the area code first.*

Gray listened to his wife slam down the phone. "I can't take this. I can't." She pressed *69 to make sure it wasn't Mrs. McCarthy.

"I'd come out there and get you, but I'm paralyzed from the neck down. Your scissor legs. I told you not to answer—it would be nothing." Gray didn't get a response, but he knew exactly what Shauna was doing, visiting her Monk Man, lighting a candle, her face glowing like a fairy. How often had he caught her staring at the painting that had belonged to her father?

Gray stayed under the bed with the comforting smell of their mixture. For a moment, he drifted, too, and imagined Mrs. McCarthy holding Audra on her shoulder in a diaper, trying to get her to burp. It's too cold for a diaper. It's fucking November. She didn't stop patting her back. Gray couldn't stand the patting, couldn't stand the old bitch's spotted face, because the baby was limp and ashen.

"Gray, can you come in here?"

His fears were confirmed. Everything was different now. He was warned by his friends who had them, and warned by his friends who didn't have them. Babies changed your life, they changed your wife. Your own mind could never relax. Because of the baby, things would never be the same. It went without saying.

"Gray, can't you come in here?"

"No. Can't you come in here and can't we do what we came here to do?" What they would always do here, Gray reminded himself, mapping things out for them, because it was not in his wife's blood to plan.

The apartment had become a very expensive mailbox since the baby was born; Shauna inherited it, but they still had to pay the maintenance every month, on top of the mortgage for the modest house, with charm, they had just bought in Larchmont. They never seemed to get the opportunity, or the energy, to use this place.

Gray realized they were slipping, turning into those Larchmont parents, the ones attached to running strollers who congregated outside Bradley's on Sunday mornings with their giant coffees, discussing elementary school academia. Soon to come: Volvo wagon; a little back fat; loss of libido (for everything except golf and weekends in Stowe); play-dates; pushing your pre-K kids—now—toward the Ivies. Chicken nuggets. The only thing Gray felt he could contribute to his community, if he was included, was his theory that the women there had no breasts.

"Gray—"

The other depressing thing he thought of was that neither one of them was as high as they were ten minutes before. He crawled out from under the bed, grabbed the joint on the bureau, heard a strand of pearls drop and roll across the floor like marbles, and headed into the living room. Gray saw his wife sitting in some kind of yoga position, the candle on the floor in front of her bare folded legs. She lifted the candle, and he stuck the joint in the flame. He dragged on the joint and handed it to Shauna. They smoked until they were in a space where there was no baby.

Gray and Shauna made love, and now he was practically examining her, kissing her under the arm with eyes open, pressing his nose there, as if this is where he might find her. He could never pinpoint her exactly, and he was afraid this was how she kept him loyal, by keeping him tangled up, never giving him enough information.

The phone rang and it was as funny as a joke. They were too tired to stand so they crawled around on their knees, which gave the night a new dimension.

"Gray, I feel syrupy—oh—there's that *ring-ring-ring* again. Sounds just like a telephone."

Gray rested on his laurels, seeing his wife finally give up the new mother act, having a good time. It was possible. They would always come here and be this way.

"Persistent caller—maybe it's The Smoker. He's at the window and sees your iridescent ass," he said.

Gray made it to his feet, walking as lightly as the first man on the moon, and stepped over to the telescope.

"I bet if we put this in the kitchen we can get into The Smoker's living room."

This would distract his wife from the sound of the phone. He stuck his eye on the lens and started skimming. The phone rang and rang.

The ringing began to lure his wife out of her high, and she looked to Gray as if she were sleepwalking toward the sound. The joy of watching her a moment ago was already bittersweet. She was on a mission now, her pure white hand already raised in front of her, moving faster. When she got to it, she put her hand on the phone and it stopped ringing. "Good. It shushed. Must have been a telemarketer."

Gray wondered how it could have been a telemarketer in the middle of the night.

Shauna stared at the phone. "Well, if it *is* Mrs. McCarthy, and it's a problem, she'll call right back—if I know *her.*"

They stayed in the same positions until enough time had passed.

"I'm going out there," she said in a song. "I'm going to find that apartment just to prove to you there is a 21X. I'm so sick of you and your know-it-all ways."

"Going out like that?"

He watched her walk out of the room and into the bedroom. When she returned she was wearing a sheer nightgown. She picked up the burning votive in front of her painting and cupped her hand around it as she walked passed him.

Gray admired his wife's face over the candle's flame, starry-eyed and provocative. She seemed to float over the floor. Had she morphed into a spirit? Sufficiently stoned now, it didn't occur to him to stop her from drifting through the hallway in that transparent nightgown.

She pulled the front door open. The sound of the hinges reminded Gray of soft-spoken angels trying to squeak out a warning. She walked out of the apartment and through the hallway.

Gray carried the leggy telescope back to the living room. He made neat piles on the cocktail table, putting all the same magazines together—*Psychology Today, Fortune, East Sider, Parents, Vogue*—and brushed off the dust. He left the dead roses in the vase. They had dried but still stood as straight as they had last spring.

Gray was startled by the sound of the phone ringing again. He felt relieved his wife was in the hall, so she wouldn't have to be sentenced to this again. Sloppily, he pushed the couch away from the wall and yanked the wire out of the socket. That's all it took. He should have done it before. Or silenced the ringer. Now, all he could hear was the faint sound of a siren from the street.

He vowed to take advantage of every moment tucked away, here, in their own clubhouse. One last spin with the telescope, a housewarming gift that had been meant for finding the Little Dipper in Larchmont. He'd promised himself earlier that he would try to find the woman who never slept. How nice it would be to see her again. Would she be dressed? Eating ice cream out of a bowl? Still high, he looked down into the lens. He searched the windows across the way, but he couldn't seem to get the focus out of his own living room. He concentrated, thinking of nothing else at that moment. Gray, with the skills of an amateur pilot flying his first night solo, couldn't find his horizon, couldn't navigate, and couldn't make a landing.

He turned his lens clockwise and counterclockwise still looking for the woman—but instead, he found a different image. The necks of two swans. One was so white and delicate, the other thick and shades darker. The image continued to blur because it was imbedded in smoke. His legs weakened as he realized he wasn't looking at the building across the way but at the building in the back, through their kitchen, and the swans were the arms of Shauna and The Smoker, their cigarettes like two beaks yapping at each other.

What were they talking about? The Smoker would be getting off on Shauna's breasts, her visible pink nipples, her starry ways. He tried to see his wife's expression through the window. The tilt of her head. He could already picture her waltzing back into the apartment, smug, without an explanation, taking her yoga position in front of her painting.

Gray raised his head from the lens. He was dizzy and nauseated; maybe he needed to eat something, but there was no food in the place. He lay down on the floor but the position did not stop his head from spinning. He closed his eyes, trying to figure out where he was. On a cold platform near the ceiling? His body felt too heavy to keep awake much longer.

The sound of the phone ringing vibrated in the center of his brain. He thought of the old cliché and how true it was— so loud it could wake the dead. Gray broke into a sweat, thinking of all the possibilities. Aware of the floor now, he began to crawl toward the phone, toward the powdery scent of their baby's head, but he fell on his back in great relief, remembering how he'd pulled the plug out.

He stretched out on the rug, still without clothes, meeting the placid eyes of the fish at Monk Man's feet. He envisioned Shauna as a little girl, sitting on the side of her father's bed, telling tales, relaying advice from the man in the painting. Gray remembered now what Shauna had told her father and how he had wished he could have been there to stop her. She had told him that Monk Man followed his craving, the darkness over his face. It freed him from the rules. Gray could see her skillfully taking the cigarette from her father's unsteady hand, putting it to her lips, then back between his fingers, without him ever realizing what she had done.

# DREAMING OVER THE MONONGAHELA RIVER

## August 1911

Lawrence Zanerdelli walked toward the Coal Queen Harbor at the far end of McKeesport, the same route he walked every morning on his way to the mines. Tonight, however, was a sticky Friday in August, eight months before he would become known as Ty. He was dressed like a gentleman enjoying a smoke on his way to make a delivery.

When Lawrence reached the receiving dock, he pulled a piece of hardened brown paper from his back pocket. It was the kind used for beef patties at the butcher—a dealer in high grade, fresh, and salt meats. (The butcher ran a clean place, thoroughly sanitary in a first-class manner). The paper had been confiscated and then decoupaged by his wife, Edda. She pasted photographs, mostly of the actress, Mary Pickford, on the meat wrappers. After painting layers of shellac over them, she hung them to dry from the crystal droplets on their chandelier, fastening them with Christmas ornament hooks.

It was startling to see the miniature, stiff bodies hanging by their heads in the quaint dining room. Lawrence never really studied Edda's craft, because his first concern had always been the wasted meat. Dr. Ramsay said to let her have her way.

Lawrence held the glistening Mary Pickford doll (Edda had a thing for the actress and tried to fix her own dry hair into the golden ringlets that Pickford was known for) and tossed it into the Monongahela River. It floated in the direction of a young couple bobbing in a rowboat with the oars tucked in, their feet in each other's laps. They were an odd addition to the scenery, which consisted of small freight boats carrying mounds of coal. He took a last drag off his cigarette and stamped it out with the ball of his foot. Lawrence wore the same elegant brown shoes, similar to the wingtips that his father wore for special occasions. He wore them today to honor the brightest idea of his life, the one sitting in his pocket.

Even though smoke from the ovens blackened everything in town, the heavy air was an escape from the sour smell in his home due to Edda's specialty—horseradish and pork knuckle. Lawrence was making his way out of the mines by working, after-hours, in his own five-and-dime store wedged in between a tavern and a miniature Russian church, which Lawrence referred to as "Onion Top Oska." To make extra money, he sold tickets in the back of the store for transportation (he catered to a certain coal baron in Smithton). His secret stash was piling up.

Lawrence sat on the bench on the dock and couldn't help looking at the woman in the boat, tossing her head back, giddy now, and wondered what it would be like to plant one on painted red lips. Instead, he pulled the envelope out of his pocket and kissed it. Holding it up to the sunlight, he traced the outline of a ship, a White Star Liner and introduced her to the sulphur polluted Monongahela. "Queen of the Ocean," he said.

The woman spotted him, and he waved the envelope at her. Her lace-up shoes were visible outside the layers and layers of her long, polka dotted dress, and he saw them as a sweet treat to be found by the tongue under so many layers of soft pastry. The man with her turned and looked, too, but Lawrence already had the envelope safely back in his breast pocket. He was thinking of the Ramsays, such fine people were Doctor Hugh, Mrs. Ramsay, and their daughter, Elizabeth. Mrs. Ramsay's father owned the Eureka Brewing Company in Smithton. The family often traveled to London and New York City to visit relatives. One could only imagine. Before their last visit to New York, Edda had presented them with a shellacked "America's Sweetheart" sprouting real hair. The silky locks were imbedded in a tiny head she must have cut from one of her old porcelain dolls.

The Ramsays were as gracious as they could be. When Lawrence arrives tonight to make his delivery, their house-keepers will be serving them dinner, arranging slices of beef in their dishes with sterling silver tongs. He had seen the wonderful extravagance on several occasions before, when he barged in on them out of desperation.

Sometimes, Lawrence ducked into Onion Top Oska to pray for God's help. Surely, he wouldn't know anyone in there. He was Catholic. What if he cried? The Zanerdelli circles under his eyes deepened every day, and Edda claimed her husband's skin was being permanently stained by the dust from the coke ovens. The Ramsays were his saviors, all the understanding they had given him over the years, the coddling of Edda. Lawrence was honored to be the only one in these parts to sell them return trip tickets from London, on the most exotic ship ever built. He marveled at the fact that he would be using such a word all the time now—*exotic.*

The couple drifted. The woman looked calm now, her foot up on the edge of the rowboat in an unladylike manner. He could see her rich brown hair pulled up neatly away from her healthy complexion. He wished he could hold her in his arms and describe to her all the fine features of his "Queen." Over forty thousand tons in all the right places. Potted shrimp for the first class. Meals served on the finest crockery. He pulled the tickets out of the envelope one last time before heading to the Ramsays and hoped the air would not discolor them.

The paper doll he'd tossed earlier floated toward the boat. Would the beauty reach out and rescue it? He read the destination on the return trip tickets out loud, as if the woman were sitting next to him on the bench, listening, her hand on his arm, attentive and focused only on Lawrence as he spoke. "En route to New York City from Southampton, England on the White Star Liner, *Titanic.*"

# TIDE POOL

# NUDES IN A GREEN POND

"Come look at the nudes, Carla." My uncle started heading toward his studio with his Chihuahua slung over his shoulder, the dog's ass snug in his fat hand. I skipped behind him, happy, cracking spearmint gum. Uncle Samson breathed with a chronic stuffy nose and dragged the heels of his feet as he walked, because he didn't have the energy or interest for either function.

"Wow," I said. I was in a sunny jungle of nudes dipped in oily color. Naked women with big brown nipples were coming at me from all directions. The unframed canvases hung in horizontal rows in a semicircle around the room like double rows of uneven teeth in a shark's mouth. Some sat very high on the walls, some low. One painting sat on an easel with a cream-colored shroud over it.

"How do you like them, Carla?" Uncle Sam shifted Teddy to the other shoulder.

"I like that one, Uncle Sam." The fumes made me careless, but I made it over to the wet canvas of the brunette nude in turquoise water up to her thighs without tripping on cans of turpentine or slipping on plastic wrappers that coated Uncle Sam's fresh Cuban cigars. "This water—it's not the same color as out back."

Uncle Samson and Aunt Henrietta lived on the harbor. At night the water looked black, and occasionally I could see a water rat's glistening back skimming the surface. There was always a slight smell of salt and fish, but the only fish I ever saw close to their house were the small minnows I caught with glass milk bottles and string right off the dock. You had to use Uncle Samson's boat, *Gone Wild*, to get to the striped bass and flounder out near Scotch Caps, the rocky area seven miles out into the Long Island Sound.

Uncle Samson rested his gooey cigar stub on the window-sill and sat down on the bench splattered with all the stunning colors that surrounded his women. Teddy got bored if he wasn't being rubbed and left the studio looking for Aunt Hen's poodle. The toy-sized dog could always be found licking her own genitalia at the foot of Aunt Hen's bed.

"Curla." Uncle Sam looked serious, the way he looked when we fished off the boat. He'd pick up the slack from his rod by instinct and just stare out on the water's surface. Waiting. I figured he shared my hopes of seeing a sleek gray fin there.

He said it again. "Curla." I never corrected his pronunciation, as I would have if he were another ten-year-old. Besides, he put a spin on all his words.

Uncle Sam lowered the music on the stereo with the most gentle fingering. He had a soft touch so it was hard for me to picture him as a boxer, but that was a long time ago, like he said. The song was familiar to me since he played it over and over while he painted with the door closed, *"Bella Maria de mi Alma"* ("Beautiful Maria of My Soul"). Then he leaned over his belly as far as he could and said without breath, "Curla... the nudes...they love to dance."

My parents were smooth dancers so I was familiar with all the actions this secret implied. Mom and Dad were elegantly romantic when they danced. They exchanged looks while they glided around, looks inspired by each other. I glanced at the nudes with thick feet.

"You mean they rumba—in there?" I wondered if they had enough room. I imagined them tumbling out of their square of canvas.

Uncle Sam got up slowly, eyeing the room for his cigar stub. He was wearing his cherry-colored bathing trunks with a terry-cloth robe draped over his shoulders. The ends of his belt dragged on the floor. He never tied anything.

"Where's Mother?" Mother was a name he called Aunt Hen. Uncle Sam was forever adjusting the windows so his studio could be filled with that southeast breeze off the harbor.

"She's on the patio with Mom and Dad. They're waiting for the fireworks. You can see 'em perfect from there."

Uncle Sam left me alone with the nudes. Most canvases held three or four women doing water ballet in a lime-green pond, or stepping out of the water, linking arms with other nudes. Two black-haired ladies faced each other in a cha-cha. Some were lounging by the grassy areas near the tropical water. A few held hands in a circle under a tree. The women looked up in a cobalt blue sky or shyly down. Their mouths were full and shocking pink. They were satisfied from the easy rhythms of their day. I could smell the flowers and mossy waters that were love seats for their bodies. One lady sat on a rock, her legs crossed, and stared at me. I knocked down a small tower of beer cans as I left the studio.

A burst of fireworks started falling slowly over the black harbor. You had to walk through Aunt Hen's living room to get to just about anywhere in the sprawling house. The picture window acted like a frame for the harbor and the patio where Aunt Hen, Uncle Sam, and my parents sat with multicolored Japanese lights strung over their heads. I could hear Aunt Hen's muffled voice from my hiding place in the living room, "Jesus Christ, Sammy!" The white poodle was in her lap, busy licking herself while Aunt Hen quickly drank her highball.

From my spot behind a massive jardinière I felt well protected from the powers in my aunt's home. Buddhas and stiff geishas proved to me you can't trust everyone in this world. All the beings here had glass eyes that followed me, even when I wasn't paying attention to them. Two Asian cats the size of German shepherds sat on each side of the china cabinet—Tom Shue's cats. Once while I played possum in the back of our car, my mom whispered to my dad, "Those Asian cats—aren't they stunning?—were a gift to Hen from that shady character, Tom Shue."

Aunt Hen kept a drawer for good girls in my favorite table, an end table standing on bird-claw legs. Inside was a copy of *The Story of Little Black Sambo*, who tried to escape the mouths of tigers by giving them his beautiful clothes. There were several trinkets from Singapore and two porcelain mockingbirds. There was an old postcard from Fiji stuck in the back of the drawer. I yanked it out and read Tom Shue's faded signature. The note smelled spicy, and I laughed when I read the closing. "Of course, my sweet and angelic Hen, I will be forever yours."

Over this end table was a rather small painting of a nude. She was different than the others in the studio. Shy maybe. A teenager? She was wet, her shiny hair dripping into a V in the middle of her back. I could see her profile, a flat nose, a full face. She was wrapping a towel around her buttocks with one leg propped up on the edge of something. I never noticed her before because a handsome Great White sat on the end table beneath her, his muscular tail bent upwards.

The screen door slapped shut, and I heard my father's footsteps. I was relieved to hear his voice. "Carla—you wanna miss the finale?" I could see the top of the dripping colors from my spot but agreed to go outside with the adults. "Dad, I'll be out in a minute. I have to get my fishing bottles ready for the morning"—cementing the fact that I would be spending the night there without my parents. I left my musty corner behind the jardinière and joined the others on the patio.

Uncle Samson explained to Teddy why the finale was "a Jackson Pollock splash." The smell of sulphur and gin was a little too much. After my father urged me outside, he wasn't even looking at the display. I climbed on my father's lap, even though I was just about too big for this sort of thing, and whispered, "Dad! The noise—it will scare the fish!" My heart broke thinking of all the plump silvery bass swimming away to other waters.

Uncle Sam said, "Curla, how do you like the fireworks?"

Aunt Hen's poodle kept yapping and quieted down only to kiss Aunt Hen under the chin with about ten licks in a row. "Sammy, get Johnny another drink here!"

I followed Uncle Sam back into the house to assist him in making a cocktail for my father. Grabbing the mermaid ice thong, I filled the glasses with ice. "Uncle Sam, the nudes, they like fishing?" I had to make sure he was planning to take me out on the boat in the morning. I could take one of the smaller portraits—the shy one—and tie her to the seat in the cabin. He could have a sandwich with her, if he wanted to. The ladies were my insurance.

"No, Curla." He dropped the cherries in the highballs. He was still wearing his trunks and robe, while everyone else was dressed. "No, the girls must be home. And, they need me first thing in the morning."

"For what?"

"Who would hold their towels for them after they bathe?"

I couldn't think of one other person who could do this job for the nudes. I started to panic thinking of our schedule for the morning—I prayed that their bathtime would be over before the tide started to go out.

We served the drinks on the patio, and my mother was giving my father a "that's enough" look. My father was egging on his cousin, as usual, getting her worked up about the stock market and real estate values where Aunt Hen made most of her money. She owned several buildings in town, one of which served as a showroom for Chryslers. Uncle Sam's job was to schmooze with customers, a job that Aunt Hen said was one that he was good for. Once, he hung a blonde nude with a pink lei around her head like a crown in the showroom over a salesman's desk, but Aunt Hen ordered it off the wall.

Uncle Sam was serving my mother with his best manners, and I was trying to prevent my mother from thinking about me going out on the boat in the morning. Mom never learned to swim or bait a hook.

"Sammy!" Aunt Hen bounced up a bit from her seat.

"Yes, Mother!" Uncle Sam bit the start of his cigar whenever Aunt Hen was about to reprimand him.

"There's no gas in the tanks, for God's sake. You're not even going to make it to the fuel dock!"

Uncle Sam watched the last explosion in the sky. "Don't worry, Mother, I'll make it."

"Jesus Christ. You should spend less time with those goddamn paint brushes and pay more attention to what needs to be done around here." Aunt Hen shooed the poodle off her lap.

My mother butted in. "There are plenty of fish right here for Carla to catch, Sam. Don't worry about getting gas. Plenty for her to do right here."

"Mom, did you bring the Wonder bread for the milk bottles?"

Fishing for minnows was depressing compared to being out on the open Sound. While I sat on the dock and stuffed bits of bread down the neck of the bottle, I always had one eye on the rocky wall that separated the harbor from the grounds of the house. Sporadically, rats ran in and out of familiar routes. Every time I ran up or down the wooden stairway that leaned against this rocky maze, I feared that one of them would nip my feet with its pin teeth. When Tom Shue visited, wearing a white suit, he made cooing noises to the rats the way Uncle Sam coaxed Teddy on his lap, but the rats never came to him.

The fireworks were over, and the sky was quiet. The audience of boats and dinghies revved up their motors and left their spots in a disorderly parade. Mom and Dad said their goodbyes. I was relieved to see my mother go before she jeopardized my early morning trip on *Gone Wild*. She pushed brown strings from my face and said, "You be good. I left the bread on the kitchen counter." I hugged my father's waist goodnight.

As I tried to fall asleep that night in the guest bedroom, I was thinking about being out on the water. It was the best feeling I had ever had. I easily jumped from the boat's upper deck to the dock and pushed us off before jumping right back on again. Uncle Sam would steer until we got out of the harbor. The best feeling started every time we left the dock as I watched the house get smaller and smaller and smaller. When the cold spray of the wake hit my face, I knew I was free.

On the way out to Scotch Caps, after Uncle Sam passed the five-mile-per-hour markers, he would hold up his hand as a sign and yell back to me, "Hold on, Curla, I'm gonna pick her up!" Usually, we passed the regulars—*Innisfree*, *Old Suzanne*, and, if Uncle Sam was having a lucky day, *Little Women*. Uncle Sam never reprimanded me, he never even tried to tell me what to do. Our jobs were cut out for us, and we worked silently alongside each other. We'd anchor and bait, fix the lures if necessary and, once in a while, exchange a dream.

"Uncle Sam? How far do you think she can go?" I asked him one day. I rubbed the teak inlays near the steering wheel as if the boat were a horse.

"As long as she can sniff her way between the rocks and keep her tail out of the mud, she can go anywhere her heart desires."

"And, as long as she has plenty of juice in the engine."

His tan face wrinkled into a frown, and then he smiled without turning in my direction. You couldn't hang around Aunt Hen without being influenced by her one way or the other.

"How about Montauk?" I unsnapped a beer for him.

"What are you dancin' around, Curla?"

"Tigers, makos…I'd even pull in a nurse. I'm not fussy."

Uncle Sam never budged. He just stared out. I didn't even push him, and he asked, "Got the stomach for chum?"

"Me?" I was game. He knew I was game. I could make a hook look like a bulky Christmas stocking the way I inserted the thing perfectly through the center of a sandworm's entire body.

When we drove back from Scotch Caps that day, Uncle Sam was thinking. He must have been charting out a route to the tip of Long Island where the ocean warmed up by the end of August. He was probably thinking of the best way to avoid those clumps of rock beneath the water that could rip your boat apart if you didn't know enough to avoid them. We'd pass Port Washington and Greenport and by the time we reached Shelter Island, we'd probably stop at one of those Dock 'n' Dine places. Finally, he'd get me to the ocean with real fish, the kind that circled their prey.

I was lost in my thoughts, too. I wanted to run through my future to the day when I would be standing on the bloody fishing docks in Montauk next to a heap of dead sharks.

The next morning I was the first one to get up and sat in the kitchen dressed for fishing. There was a naked girl hanging on the wall over the pine table. She was sitting on a bench with her back facing me, but she managed to look over her shoulder. A basket of odd shaped apples sat next to her.

Uncle Sam joined me for breakfast. He still wore his terry-cloth robe, and his hair was wet. His face flushed as he searched for fruit in the refrigerator and found a mango that was already peeled.

"Everyone have their bath, Uncle Sam?" I was hopeful that his services for the nudes were over and done with and that we could get on with our day's activities.

I recognized the sounds of Aunt Hen's Italian bracelets so I was prepared for her entrance. She came rushing into the kitchen wearing her full-length satin robe. A Japanese maple tree sprang from the bottom of the robe and fanned out across her broad shoulders.

"Sammy, Carla will wait here with me while you go to the fuel dock—and have them check that motor again!"

Uncle Sam left the kitchen without any comment, and I was hoping he wasn't going to close himself in his studio. If he did we'd never make it out to Scotch Caps before the tide went out. I suggested to Aunt Hen that I was going to remind him about getting to Rosie's Bait and Tackle Shop for the sandworms. Rosie always had just one box of sandworms left in her fridge every time we went to buy them.

Aunt Hen drank her tea standing up and said, "Honey, I think his boxing days have taken their toll on Uncle Sammy. He can't breathe right from taking punches, but it's his brain that's stuffed up."

It sounded like she added, "That chooch."

After I knocked on the studio door several times, Uncle Sam and Teddy let me in.

*"Quiereme mucho"* ("How Much Do You Want Me?") was playing too loud for my ears. He had Teddy on his left shoulder while he rubbed some finishing touches on the nude that had been under a shroud last night.

Teddy squirmed down to the floor and tested me for a rub, but I was concerned about the tide. I could feel a nice strong wind even in the studio. "Uncle Sam?"

His thumb and forefinger were coated in pinks and flesh tones. He didn't have his painting clothes on, but he wiped his hands on his sides anyway.

I picked up an old rag with turps and dark paint on it and offered it to him. "Don't you think we better get going? I mean, it's getting late and the last time we got out to Scotch Caps I said we were lucky with all the bites and you said that timing was everything."

"Bullseye, little Curla." He didn't take his eyes off his work-in-progress. "See her? She's just about to show me her charms." He stood back and admired that one. "Let me finish up, Curla, then I'll change for the trip."

I walked back through the living room to the kitchen and stopped to look at Tom Shue's cats since the morning light gave me a different outlook on things. I heard Aunt Hen's teacup hit the saucer every once in a while, and I figured I might as well get her going about Tom Shue to get her mind off lazy Uncle Sam—but she wasn't the type of lady to forget anything.

"Tommy Shue?" She put her teacup in the sink like she was fed up with it. She lowered her voice, and it startled me as much as if she had screamed. "Honey, all men are the same—with the exception of my Tommy."

Just the sight of me in my fishing gear must have reminded her about the gas, and I could see her pale cheeks come to
life with anger. Uncle Sam told me repeatedly while teaching
me to troll that his wife was full of piss and vinegar.

I picked up the teacup to distract her and held it in front
of my face. She grabbed it from me and said, "No, honey,
put it up to the sunlight." She held the teacup high in front
of the sunny window and put a spoon behind it with the
other hand. "Now, look, Carla, if you can see right through
china—see?—you've got yourself the real thing."

It was getting hot now, and my plan to fish off the boat
rather than the lousy dock out back was making me desperate. "I better get the buckets and stuff out of the shed, Aunt
Hen." I was sweaty and wanted to be out of there.

I followed the worn Persian rug through the narrow hallway to the studio on the other side of the house. When I got
there I thought I must have been in the wrong room, but
it smelled right. The door stood open, and the breeze was
blowing the sheer curtains into the room. I could hear calm
waves hitting the sides of the dock. A single canvas rested on
an easel in the center of the studio. Teddy sat on the floor,
abandoned.

"Teddy? Where is everyone? Where are the nudes—and
Uncle Sam?"

Uncle Sam was nowhere to be found. Only his robe re-
mained, bunched up on the splattered workbench, dirty with
oils. I could smell fresh paint and the yellowy linseed oil he
always worked with.

I went to the open window and looked out on the boat. I
didn't see any sign of Uncle Samson. Usually, just before we

left for a couple of hours of fishing, he would fool with the motor and check things on board.

I wondered if my mother had found out about the trip to the Caps and had nixed my fun the way she often did. I stood there too frustrated to even cry. I had prepared sandwiches and brought sodas and beer. I gave Teddy a rub. His eyes looked more crusty than usual.

A whiff of salt water blew in, reminding me that had I been on the boat with Uncle Sam, my line would be cast and I'd be ready for a good-sized bass to come my way. There was nothing like a nice swift jerk of the line when you knew you had one.

I stood in the center of the studio, staring at the one canvas left in the room. The oils on it were wet and because of the glare I went up to it as close as I could. At first, all I noticed were the muted colors, unlike the sharp hues and flatness of Uncle Sam's paintings. This one was amazingly different. A Florentine table was in the middle of the scene with a very large man standing on top of it. I wondered if the table might break. The man was naked, just like the women off to the sides of the picture peeking at him from behind the trees. He had one leg up a little bit--he was dancing. In fact, he was in a spin. His face was a blur, but I could tell he was happy.

# CROWDED POND

"You spoiled little darlings!" Harley had that hand-on-your-hip kind of attitude when it came to her pets. She gave them everything and then fretted that they were too pampered.

"If I didn't love you so much, I'd eat you all up!" She lifted the lid off the sugar bowl and the buggers were already piling on top of one another, crawling toward Harley's voice. Eight fat black ants. Big ones as far as ants go.

Harley's husband, Orson, stood in the kitchen doorway with his wet suit on.

"There's bread for toast," Harley offered with her back to Orson, while Duffy inched up her forefinger.

Orson flip-flopped through the moss-colored kitchen. He seemed unsure of which direction to turn. "No time. The Turner pond today. Thirty-four koi." The screen door slammed behind him but didn't latch. Orson forgot something, as usual, and poked his rubber-coated head through the kitchen window. "My mask?"

"Check the trunk." With satisfaction, Harley watched Orson's clumsy gait disappear as he was vacuumed by the early fog.

Harley figured the Turner fish were already dead. She learned from hearing Orson's expertise gnawing at his brain in the middle of the night. Nightmares of fish overload caused him to mumble in his sleep: *A crowded pond leads to*

135

*suffocation.* Sometimes Orson would kick off the sheets and make his way to the bathroom. Harley would find her husband on the cold floor clawing the bottoms of his dirty feet, always making the same observation to himself: *Sandworms? I'm gonna pick you out, you little fuckers!* Harley chalked this up to all that booze he guzzled nightly at the Tank Top Bar.

Harley stood in the breakfast nook with fists as tight as clams. "I turn away for one second and you're all over the place!" The slow ants spread out, roaming the humid kitchen. Duffy was on the floor sniffing a piece of silt from Orson's slimy flipper. Marcus was stuck in grout.

The phone rang.

"Yes?" Harley answered the phone this way. Whoever was calling could get right to it.

"I'm looking for Orson—Orson's Pond Service. We're breeding our koi. We heard Orson's the best at this sort of thing."

"Your problem?" Harley looked for a pen, one eye on her clan running in all directions, fading into dots. Her forehead was moist from motherly rage.

The customer babbled with compassion. "Well, we've done everything. You know, for breeding. We throw them chop-meat, flies, bits of hot dogs. I read sound husbandry is the key. You heard that?"

Harley had had it. The oddball on the phone was worried about her fucking fish while Duffy was disappearing under the refrigerator.

Harley made a double knot with the green telephone wire and threw the receiver into the vase of old daisies. It sunk to the bottom in the aging water.

Harley stepped back without looking and heard a crunch. Marcus. She wiped him off her flat heel and smeared him on the counter. Fed up with their antics, Harley ran after Duffy and the others and stomped on all of them. She scraped them up with a butter knife and rubbed them into the mortar.

The screen door bounced without closing and Orson stood in the doorway. "It's not there. I might have left it at the shop." Orson moved toward his wife, giving her a little shove out of the way. As he passed her he yanked her elbow toward him then he let it go as if her limb were a catch not worth keeping.

Harley detested his uncertainties, his cowardice, his morning smell.

Orson slowly hoisted himself on top of the green Formica counter next to the sink and placed his open mouth under the faucet for a drink of water.

Harley returned to her job at the mortar and pestle and ground her darlings to a soft black paste with a splash of water. "Time for toast now? I've got some fresh blackberry jam."

Orson moved into his favorite chair at the kitchen table and sat there with a know-it-all attitude on his face, like some kind of fish scientist. He tapped his finger and waited for Harley to serve him breakfast.

# MUST BE NEAR THE HUDSON

Nell was in the shower, a makeshift shower similar to a large plastic container shoved into the corner of the bathroom. She reached for the shampoo and knocked the bottle of "Scent Off" from the shelf. The top popped, and the smell of artificial pine trees filled the stall. She stuck her nose outside the plastic shower curtain for fresh air. She heard the voice of the Scranton news anchor on the TV in the bedroom. It was six a.m., September 10, 2001, the first bead in a string of beautiful fall days. The cream on top of all this blue sky? Troy was leaving, on the sly, to head to the Ruby Range to catch another one of his Bullwinkles.

A breeze caused the cold shower curtain to stick to her body. Nell figured if she stayed in the shower long enough, Troy might be gone by the time she got out. He was going on the Q.T. from the plant, because he didn't have any vacation time left. She heard him on the phone, calling in sick with an early flu that would keep him out for several days.

Nell looked forward to her time alone. She was going to bang away on her upright, make cheesy olives, have her friends over for sangria with chopped up fruit. When she greets the customers at Wal-Mart, no one will be asking her about her unhappy face. With Troy in the pristine and untouched, there will be a salve in her joints as she fetches carts, checks receipts, eyes the shoplifters eyeing the goods,

138

and give them her Nelliest of looks. How often she gave customers an ear, listened to a request that bloomed into a problem sister-in-law, a sick spouse. It was surprising the conversations she found herself in, the advice she offered. Her talent to assist and heal came from experience: she considered herself an expert on suffering.

Soaping up her leg for a shave, she imagined Troy being dropped by an inexperienced bush pilot—who he would pay cash to, for secrecy—while out in the remote and rugged. An unguided hunt, the way he liked it. She saw him hunched over a fire with a small tin pot of beans, nestled in some God-forsaken mountain range, wolf, wolverine, black bear, and caribou just hundreds of feet away.

Now, in the strip of space between the shower curtain and plastic wall, Troy searched under the sink, slapping bottles out of the way, reaching for the Imodium. His stomach was as sensitive as a baby's. He stood up slowly, getting off one knee, then the other and turned around, so much like a grizzly she wondered how she never saw the likeness before. She stuck her head back in and watched the shadow of his mass approach.

He pushed the curtain aside. "I'm leaving in ten," he said, his stutter temporarily gone. "For all you know, I have the flu so bad I can't get my head off the pillow. If any shithead asks."

"Will do, but I'm freezing my bahoongas off." Nell pulled the curtain closed.

Troy opened it just as fast. He came in, bare chested, his sweats on, the tiniest beads of water in between the hairs of his beard. He pressed his thumb on the top of her arm.

"P-P-Powerful," he said, patting the backs of her arms, her thighs, the parts he loved to pick-on. His hands smelled like the oily solution from his 300 Magnum.

Nell believed Troy's lifetime of stuttering had turned him into a bully, low self-esteem and all that. Classic case but she didn't care enough to read up on it. Kind of too late. He undid his pants and lifted her slightly so he could get himself inside her. The floor buckled and surely the shower would topple over with their overweight selves.

When he was done, he pulled his feet out of his sopping pants and left them in the stall. He walked over to the sink, wiped all of himself with the face cloth, grabbed the box of Imodium, and started down the hall.

"Don't forget, Neller. Don't forget what I told you to say. Only if asked."

"Flu, flu, flu. Can't get your head up. Stuck to the pilla," she said, her head sticking out of the curtain the way an actress does in those old movies, with the steam around her heart-shaped face. She studied the trail of water as she pressed the palm of her hand on her breast to cushion the throbbing.

Years ago, after Nell had her last miscarriage, she and Troy had been driving home from the hospital when she asked him what was so great about traipsing around in the middle of nowhere? *Neller, all your s-s-senses get into the act. I can't do the words right, but it's all so untouched—a small Outfitter's Super Club--at l-l-less than one thousand feet—the s-s-sound of it flying is so g-g-god damn obvious. Even a f-f-frog rubbing his fucking legs is obvious. And, the wolves, the sound of them h-h-howling at night slices right through you.* It had taken him forever to get it out, just like Nell had planned. She'd needed to zone out after all she had been through, so she had asked him a question about the only subject that was of interest to him, the only thing he would talk about. Nell thought stutterers were just plain old antisocial and that's why Troy liked being in the middle of nowhere.

The next morning Nell felt the excitement walking into Wal-Mart, getting ready for her day that would just get better, returning home that night to friends and sangria. Maybe it was the lighting, like a casino, the jingles and noise.

"Hey Sebastian, party at my house tonight," she sang over to him.

She had gotten to know Sebastian through the "mock" shoplifting night for employees. Sebastian made most of the announcements over the speakers with his old DJ voice. That's what she liked about this greeter job, people like him, people you could talk to, get real deep with. Wal-Mart's fluorescent lights were turning her on from the inside, right around the valves of her heart.

She found a little girl watching all the televisions. "Who are you with, you little Gretel?" The girl looked up and raised her hands. She must have been about five. Nell, surprised, picked her up. One of the service skills she had learned in the training seminar was to be proactive rather than reactive, and this kid needed her. The little girl pointed to the TV and soon all the customers were crowding the aisle, watching the special broadcast. Nell looked at the customers' faces, not being a TV addict herself, and knew something was very wrong.

Sebastian came to Nell and put his arm around her and the girl as the reports showed the United States under attack in New York City. "Must be the Middle East," he said, his eyes fixed on the screen.

The first of the Twin Towers at the World Trade Center started to collapse. Nell pressed the child's face into her shoulder so she wouldn't see people jumping from the windows.

Nell was determined to keep her head during the chaos, as customers ran out of the store and into their cars. It was her job, and more importantly, despite the confusion, she had a lost little girl to return to her parents. She found Sebastian and asked him to make an announcement about the lost girl. How could her parents not be frantic? Especially now? With all the sudden noise, would the announcement be heard? The little girl was so darling, so ready to be Nell's friend. She sat with the girl in the waiting booth for her parents to come and claim her. In Nell's old imagination, she saw herself as queen and the girl as her princess daughter, overlooking a kingdom in turmoil.

Nell closed her eyes to block out the horror depicted on every single television in the store. And, with her eyes shut, she saw Troy, alone in the Ruby Range. She couldn't tell anyone he was there because she was under strict orders. Within an hour of the attacks, the FAA had reported that all airports were shut down and all air traffic was halted nationwide. Would everything go back to normal, or was this the end of the world? If anyone asked, she would just say Troy had abandoned her.

Sitting in the waiting booth, the girl on the miniature chair next to her, Nell imagined Troy opening his mouth, unable to get a word out. Could he sense that all was too quiet? That he may never be picked up? She thought about the string on his sweatpants that was never tied, his beard that needed to be trimmed, the small box of anti-diarrhea medicine, the three emergency ration bars, two thousand four hundred calories each, the wolverines and Dall's sheep, moose, and bear. And, how a pack of wolves howling in the mountains can really break the silence of the wilderness.

# TWO PIGS AND A CIRCLE OF PALM TREES

Mingo was always spoiling Pita with little gifts and brought her two baby pigs, which she immediately grabbed from him without saying thank you. Pita never said thank you because she believed that actions spoke much louder than words, and placed the sucklings in the bidet, handling them like two glass eggs. She turned the faucet on just a touch, and the pigs nuzzled each other, nose to ass, belly to belly. Pita kissed the speck of dried blood on Mingo's cheek and whispered, "Now I have my own little sausages."

Pita wasn't afraid to take the pigs out in the heat without lathering them in sunscreen, because the house Mingo and Pita shared was shaded by a circle of palm trees. The trees stood like crooked birthday candles on the rim of a cake. Pita sat in a wicker chair she had bought at the Boynton Beach flea market, with Spoon and Mooch in her arms, and watched Mingo on the sunny side of the yard, oiled and hunched over. She couldn't see her favorite part of his body, his middle-aged belly, one that matched her own. His hands were deep in a large crate. Pita got that afraid feeling again, and pulled the pigs closer to her breasts.

Spoon and Mooch had become noisy since they arrived and squealed constantly. They squirmed and squealed and wiggled right out of Pita's arms and ran straight for the pool, as if they were going to do cannon balls off the side, one after the other. Mingo had the small portable TV outside, plugged into the outlet for the electric barbecue they never used. The Palm Beach County News was on. No matter where he was, indoors, outdoors, in the car, on the boat, Mingo had the local news blaring.

Pita ran past the darting pigs and belly-flopped into the pool so small that by the time she came up for air, she was already on the other side. Spoon and Mooch were behind her in the pool, bobbing up and down, doing the dog paddle, their smooshed-in faces looking desperate to stay above water.

Pita called for Mingo. His slick back was free of any freckles and he was wearing a bikini bathing suit in neon green. Mingo was still working on whatever he was working on, shaking his head at reports that two drug traffickers from Dixie had been caught while speeding on their boat on the Intracoastal. "Assholes," Mingo said with a cigarette hanging out of his mouth. Boxes and boxes of Ziploc bags Pita picked up for him with coupons at Publix were piled on the ground next to his bare feet.

Pita screamed at Mingo's narrow ass, which faced her. "My piggies are drowning!" She swam a beautiful breaststroke directly to Spoon and Mooch, scooped them up, and placed them on the broken concrete. The pigs, squeaking, took off after the little lizards and disappeared in the hedges.

Mingo grabbed a towel with some grass stuck to it and wiped his hands. His black curls were so black she could see moving streaks of blue in them as they fell on his shoulders. The tips of his hair were greasy.

Mingo's work area was spread out over the old picnic table left by the family that used to live there. Surveying his packages, he sang back to Pita, as if he didn't hear her request, in his usual lovey-dovey way, "Hey baby, what can I do to you?" He said it like the bartender, their friend Dag, who worked down at The New Taboo. They were always imitating Dag in the mornings, sashaying around their one bedroom, unkempt house that smelled like an orange grove. Sometimes they imitated Dag so much they forgot their own voices and expressions.

Mingo, who didn't let too many minutes go by without showing Pita some affection, came to her, knelt down at the edge of the pool and slid a kiss on her grape-colored lips.

It was natural for Mingo and Pita to make love right out in the back yard in the sun on the beach chair that had missing slats in the seat area. Pita's heavy bottom would bounce on the ground with each thrust. Or, they would do it on the steps of the pool in shallow water, oblivious to the slapping noises they made. Now Pita was more concerned about the pigs' whereabouts. Like children, if they were too quiet, she figured they must be in trouble.

Mingo helped his love out of the pool and watched her on the prowl. Now she was half in a bush, half out, calling for the "scampers," a name Mingo had given them so easily as soon as they arrived.

"Hey," Mingo yelled after Pita, a little miffed at her diverted attention. "I got to get somethin' in my stomach. Let's go down to The Clam Trap."

"Spoon and Mooooch!" Pita called, as if she was playing hide-and-seek, her thick-skinned body getting scratched. She emerged from the bushes with the pinkish pigs, now spotted with grape-colored lips marks. She was afraid of Mingo's re-action, but she said it anyway. "What am I going to do while we're out? Tie them up on leashes?"

The couple left the pigs in the leaking bidet in their tur-quoise bathroom, with the door closed and the window open, while they went to the restaurant for lunch. Pita left a loud ticking clock wrapped in a soft blanket so that Spoon and Mooch could snuggle next to a beating heart.

Pita did all the driving because Mingo's eyes were always looking in the rearview mirror, or his side mirror, or at the low flying helicopters—never on the road in front of him. She felt generous being Mingo's driver. It was just another way for her to relax him and make him realize that when you really love someone, you put yourself out.

When Pita drove Mingo around West Palm, she noticed the people at the corner stops. She never pointed them out to Mingo, he had so much on his mind. From behind the wheel, she looked for them on certain corners, the way one looks at the same condemned house on the daily route to work. The bus stoppers always looked too hot or too tired to speak to one another, the same expression on each face, peering down the road. They reminded her of the basket of unmatched socks in her closet, worn-out socks that would never have mates. If Mingo were a different sort, even if he was just a little sociable or talkative, she would have stopped to ask one if he or she needed a lift. But all she could do was say "thank you" in her heart. She had a real love in her life; this was her fortune.

The Clam Trap was an outdoor restaurant on the inlet with old rotting buoys hanging from the ceiling—the old lighted whistle kind, or the bell types, and the ones that look like cans that rattled so loudly before a storm, the customers at the bar had to raise their voices to be heard.

Pita and Mingo sat at "their" table in the darkest corner of the lounge area, where they were still able to order certain items off the menu. Pita was adrift in the book-like menu, scanning over endless choices. Mingo waved to the waitress to give them more time as he watched her slowly turn the pages back to the beginning. "Just get whatever you want" was all he ever said when she got like that. Finally, she decided on fried clam sandwiches with batter-dipped onion rings, served in small plastic baskets. She glanced around at the orders being placed on the tables and wondered if she had made the right decision.

After lunch, Pita was stuffed and anxious to get home to her pets. The snap on her shorts was digging into her belly-button, and by instinct Mingo, put his hand under her shirt and unsnapped them. His fingers quickly slid down and into her vagina through the tight space between her inner thigh and shorts, and then he went right back to his cigarette. It comforted him to see Pita full and satisfied. He imagined a man could feel that way watching his children.

Mingo held up his beer mug to the waitress and nodded.

"Oh, come on. Let's get outta here. I'm bustin'," Pita whined. Her lips were shiny and natural from the onion rings cooked in corn oil. She knew she'd feel even better if she could just check the pigs and screw around with Mingo for the rest of the afternoon.

"Hey, man." Mingo jumped up and slapped his friend Jon on the back who called him whenever he got a roofing or siding job. The two men, who looked like twins, hooked each other around the neck and walked over to the bar area. Pita waited, antsy in her seat.

Mingo and Jon now stood at the bar, talking real low and looking up at the television. The buoys really rattled; even the ones inside the lounge area were swaying. Outside, lightening flashed and the smell of fish blew in from the docks.

On the way back to their house, Pita and Mingo got caught in the thunderstorm, and Pita could barely see the road in front of her. The rain banged so hard on the convertible roof, Mingo had to turn up the news to the loudest volume.

"What's going on?" Pita asked Mingo without taking her eyes off the road. She was thinking of him and Jon, up at the bar, whispering, clearly in cahoots with each other.

"Nothing, babe."

"I'm not stupid, you know. What were you talking about— one of your special deals?"

"No deals." He oomphed his words and bulged his eyes like she did. "He's got another job for me."

"Oh, a job. A real one like mine."

"No, I'm not a cashier chick. I lay flat roofs. I smear tar. I burn my ass laying those rolls. You care."

"Yeah. Looks to me like you do all your smearing in the middle of the night."

"Ask Jon. It's a commercial roof—on Clematis Street, on that new mall."

"Really?"

"Really. As soon as we've got the fuckin' materials I can get started."

Pita was satisfied for the time being. She looked at Mingo

next to her; he was simmering down. When you have more to love, she thought, you have more to lose.

Mingo rubbed her thigh while she drove, squeezing a handful of her leg. "I want some stuff like that there," he said, using Dag's twang and phrase for a good-looking woman.

Even though Pita couldn't see beyond the windshield through the hard rain, she knew the temperament of Florida's weather. The predictability was a comfort to her. In just a few minutes the storm would stop, and she would be driving on a sunny, wet boulevard back to their home.

Mingo held the door for Pita, so she was the first to see the damage when she walked in the house. Pita smelled cigar smoke, a smell that made her think of her father, even though she couldn't remember his face. The dirt from the spider plants was flung all over the small living room. The television screen was smashed in, every drawer was removed, emptied, and thrown across the room.

"Dumb fucks," Mingo said over his shoulder. "Like they're gonna find a sweet stash." He headed toward the back door.

Pita ran after Mingo and jumped on his back. She dug her nails in his fatty shoulders. He seemed more shocked at her clawing his skin than he had been walking into his own torn-apart home.

Mingo pulled Pita off him. He held her two wrists together with one hand. He turned her body around holding her firmly from behind, his mouth next to her ear.

"Want me?" He forced her down by pressing on her shoulders.

"What the hell is going on? I guess we got ripped up here

because of your roofing job?" She was on her knees, her face spotted with mascara. She loved him so much. "You're gonna end up in jail again."

"Oh, you're different than me? Your ass ain't clean either. Do I give a shit?"

Pita didn't say anything.

Mingo bent down to her, held her jaw, and kissed her on the mouth. "So, if the cops are after me, I'll hide out for a while." He let her go and walked out the back door, into the yard.

Inside, Pita sat down on the heap of couch cushions. Her legs were shaking. She was surrounded by dirt all over the floor. "Oh God!" She jumped up and ran to the bathroom.

The pigs were under the old rags, snuggled next to the alarm clock. Pita forgot everything for the moment and held the pigs in her arms.

The doorbell was ringing. Pita answered the door, without hesitation, without looking through the peephole. With Spoon and Mooch in her arms, she opened the door and saw Dag standing there. His red hair was greased into a croissant on top of his head.

"Come on in," she said, her whole body swaying a bit for the pigs, in a rhythm much like Dag's walk.

"Look at this place—friend of yours stop by?" Dag talked with a lisp, one that Mingo and Pita couldn't get down just right when they imitated him.

"I guess we need new friends."

"Oh no!" Dag ducked, raising his elbows to make a shield, fooling around like he was afraid of wild beasts. "It's…it's… the scampers!"

Pita pushed him out of the way, trying not to smile.

"Where's your old man?" Dag gave Pita's ass a quick round rub.

"Out back."

While the two men were in the backyard, Pita cleaned slowly. Stopping for a cigarette, watching the pigs play in the dirt from the overturned plants, she realized that the cops would never stop coming after them. They were going to hunt them down, because her new life with Mingo was too good to be true.

The doorbell rang again and Pita answered. Two cops, in plain clothes that were more like a uniform than an actual uniform, pushed themselves in. One of them pinned her up against the wall and held her there with his left hand around her neck, the other on her breast.

"Where is he?" the cop asked, his lower lip practically touching Pita's nose.

"Look at these things," the other cop said as he kicked one of the pigs across the room. It smashed into the wall, the small head cracked like an egg, oozing down to the floor.

"You son of a bitch!" Pita yelled. The cop who was pinning her down nailed her stomach with his knee. She wailed and moaned, looking at the dead pig, the blood around his ear. She could see his face, his bottom jaw pushed up and out. How pathetic. Her baby. She wanted to hold him. She prayed and prayed right there that fear would make Spoon hide.

The cop who had killed the pig was now searching through the house, while the cop holding Pita whispered the same question in her ear. His hand was over her mouth now.

"Where is he?"

"Out back."

Pita, relieved that Mingo could smell cops, knew by now he would be gone. He'd always said he had radar for officers; she was in there stalling, taking their shit, so he had time to run. His spare car was always parked on the corner of Federal and Flamingo Drive, so that he could get away.

The cop let her go and followed the other cop out the back door.

Pita was confident that Mingo had escaped. She stood up and felt a searing pain in her abdomen. She found Spoon under the cushions and hugged him, wailing again. She couldn't bear to look at Mooch now. She would always remember the death in his face and his mushy body twisted unnaturally on the floor.

Pita carried Spoon into the kitchen. She lit a cigarette with her trembling free hand. She watched the two cops from the window as they snooped around the yard in their Hawaiian colored clothes. The portable TV was so loud that one of the cops kicked it off, the same one that had kicked her baby into the wall. After they gave up their search, they hopped over the fence and disappeared.

Pita rubbed Spoon in the soft spot under his chin, in the tuft of white hair. She put the radio on in the kitchen and turned up the volume and, like a burning candle, kept vigil for her man. Pita didn't hear the music. She was reminiscing. Mingo used to surprise her by filling the bidet with ice and champagne. They'd take the cold bottle and plastic cups out into the backyard at night, stuff themselves into one beach chair, smoke a joint, and get a little drunk.

Pita ran the faucet and poured herself a glass of water. She looked into the bottom of the glass for a few moments, then drank slowly, feeling the water run over her tender insides. At Publix, where she worked, people bought huge jugs of spring water, and each time she scanned for the price, the extravagance of it stunned her. Now, she couldn't stand the rustiness of the Florida water she had lived with all her life.

Without letting go of the pig, Pita went into the bedroom and packed a denim suitcase: earrings, underwear, bras, a few halter sundresses, make-up, and nail glue. She had strappy sandals on, the only shoes she would need. She lay down on the bed with Spoon and let him lick her toes. She cried again because, for a moment, she thought it was Mooch's little sandy tongue licking away. He had been the timid one.

The smell of oranges reached her for the first time all day. "Time to go, little sausage." She got up, placed the pig on her shoulder and walked out the back door with her suitcase.

Pita tried to remember where the bus stop was. She walked down Federal and noticed the short row of faces she used to watch from the car as she drove Mingo around. She got in line at the bus stop with her companion and whispered in his triangular ear, "We won't let a man like that go, will we?" If the shoe had been on the other foot, Mingo would find her, probably sneak up behind her with a treat for her in his hand. It was the only thing in life she was sure of.

Pita stepped onto the bus, avoiding the faces staring at her and the bundle cradled in her left arm. She wobbled a little on her heels, trying to balance everything along with Spoon. Two teenaged boys wearing netted T-shirts spit *oink-oink, grunt-grunt* noises at her. One of them put his foot across the aisle so she couldn't walk further. The other boy in the seat behind his friend put his foot up so she couldn't step back. The boy in front of her focused on her breasts, parting his lips. She didn't look into his eyes. Instead, she settled on the size of his arms, the dark nipples through the openings of his shirt. She pushed her knee forward to break the barrier and the boy laughed and pulled it away. "Stupid cunt," he said, turning to his friend. Pita lost her balance but managed to keep herself upright before falling into the first available seat. Spoon let out a new sound from the strength of Pita's grip. The other passengers sat quietly.

Once Pita felt able, she got up, found an empty seat in the back, and settled in. Pita knew the cops would find Mingo, or he would find them. He had prepared her for what might happen. She knew where to look. She rocked Spoon dreamily, unable to look into his glassy eye slivers.

When the bus stopped in traffic near the entrance to the Rain or Shine Flea Market, it felt to Pita as though they would be stuck on Federal Highway for the rest of their lives. She smelled the rain coming and looked up to see storm clouds blowing ahead. She imagined the waves at Delray Beach and the scattered palm trees being sucked down by the wind.

Pita crouched down with Spoon in the torn seat and opened a bag of chips she had brought from home. As the bus finally started to roll, she watched the scenery. She could predict every site coming up—Hula Girls' Tiki Bar, the Used-Cars-4-U! lot with all the streams blowing like they were having a sale, the new pink mall. She picked up Spoon and held him up in front of the window for a moment, so he could see the main drag. His hind feet dangled until he squirmed to get back into Pita's lap. As the bus made a sloppy turn onto A1A, she watched people running off Delray Beach, dragging sand chairs and coolers. She noticed how disgusted they looked, as if they were forced into traffic by waves escaping the Atlantic. Big deal, it's only rain, Pita thought as the road began to clog. She sank into her seat and the bus came to a dead stop.

# WHITE CAPS

# THE WATER IN
# ALEXANDER'S EYES

Every time one of the third graders vomited, Mrs. Knick-erbocker threw a handful of granules over the mess and waited for Vinny, the janitor, to come in and mop it all up. We were never quite sure what the granules did, besides blanketing one smell on top of another, but no one could get their minds off the thing until Vinny showed up to do his job. These kinds of events never stopped Mrs. Knickerbocker from chattering, she simply rearranged the desks around the spot like it was just another third grader at St. Peter's. Straightening us into new rows with her meaty arms, she pushed Alexander Lamb's desk smack-up next to mine. Now the two of us sat directly under the chipped statue of Mary the Blessed Virgin. The statue with the honest face was about the size of a toddler. I turned to Patty O'Mahoney behind me to make sure she saw my new desk-mate, to acknowledge that the secrets I shared with her about Alexander and fate were true. But she was busy sniffing the fresh purple ink off the photocopied paper with her eyes closed.

When the three o'clock bell rang, the vomit was still on the floor. We all ran out of the classroom with that cheesy smell in our noses and rushed down the stairway to the back exit. I found Vinny the janitor on the far side of the playground near the old bicycle racks, his foot inserted where a couple of iron bars were missing. He was smoking a cigarette.

"Hey, Vinny—no smoking allowed." It was my way to boss.

His shoulders shot up at the sound of my voice. Even though I had startled him he turned around slowly, the dark circles under his eyes making me think of Halloween.

"It's Miss Olivia de Havilland."

"It's not Olivia de Havilland! It's Olivia Darnell! And Mrs. Knickerbocker is angry with you!"

Vinny inhaled like he was never going to stop and rubbed the stubble on his cheek with a crooked thumb. He was creepier outdoors than indoors, and now I could really see that the whites of his eyes were yellow like pee.

"Mrs. Knickerbooper is angry with me? Oh, no she's not. She thinks I'm a faithful janitor. Ya know something? I'm going up to her classroom right now." Vinny stamped his unfinished cigarette into the concrete with a smile. I watched him put a peppermint in his mouth and smooth down his oily hair.

"Well, Vinny, don't forget your mop! And, it's Mrs. Knickerbocker, not Mrs. Knickerbooper!" After he left, I picked up his half-smoked cigarette and slipped it under the flap of my bookbag.

On the way home I caught up with Patty O'Mahoney. Patty was frail. She wore several layers of clothing, because her mother worked at a florist in town. She spent many after-school hours watching her mother arrange bouquets in the coolers. If Patty didn't go to my house after school, she walked directly to the shop. Patty was a believer. Once I confided to her on the way home from St. Peter's that the Beatles were using our garage to practice their songs—they were

159

using it as a hideout. Patty wore an "I Love Paul" button on her first layer of clothing next to her heart.

Today I had more secret information for her.

Patty talked while walking, never diverting from her route. "Olivia—wanna come to the shop with me? My mom's getting ready for Valentine's Day—it's her busiest time—she'll let us stick the lovebirds in the dirt." Patty wore very thick glasses so her eyes looked as big as ping pong balls.

"Can't—I gotta go home. Alexander is coming over tonight, and we're going to smoke a cigarette."

I was surprised at Patty's silence. Perhaps she was suspicious, so I took out the flattened cigarette from my bookbag. I licked it and rolled it between my fingers to plump it up. We stopped at the intersection where Patty was supposed to make her turn up the hill to the florist. I handed my treasure to Patty, but she wouldn't take it.

"Does Alexander know how to smoke?" she asked.

"Yes, his brother taught him."

"Where are you going to do it?"

"In the garage."

"What about the Beatles? They'll see. They'll tell your mother!"

"Oh, they smoke all the time."

"Your mother's going to kill you, Olivia. My mother said your mother is a proper lady. My mother said she doesn't know how such a lady has a little girl like you."

Before I left Patty, worried and fretting on the corner, I wrapped the good-sized butt in a piece of loose-leaf paper and pushed it to the bottom of my book bag.

My mother was a proper lady. And, she was fancy. Every morning I stood on top of the toilet bowl and stared out into the gardens while she weaved glossy ribbons through my black French braid, or pulled back all my hair in a tight ponytail with a velvet bow. Other mothers did these things on holidays or Sundays, but this was just part of my mother's daily morning routine, like making toast was for others. My father usually appeared in the bathroom to say goodbye while my hair was being done, leaning his cheek my way to accept a kiss if I was fast enough. I watched my parents look into each other's eyes every morning at this moment and witnessed my family in the bathroom mirror. My mother's reflection was always a frown, since my father's starched collars were never stiff enough for her approval.

I particularly enjoyed watching my mother's ceremony of dressing on Saturday evenings. Everything she wore, every piece of jewelry she put on, had a legend to go with it. The clump of diamonds on her pinky were engagement rings handed down to her from her great-grandmother. Even the diamond my father gave her was buried in the setting. Mother had all the diamonds made into one cocktail ring. She would hold out her stark white manicured hands and say, "Olivia, this is our heritage."

When I came home from school my mother was usually out at her Women's Club or lunching in New York for various social causes. She told me many times over the phone while I did my homework, "My heart goes out to these people." And, she would sigh dramatically as she did for everything important and unimportant. Mother always said, "Bye, bye love," before she hung up, and, "Listen to Bernadette."

Bernadette was our "good soul" who lived in our home and made our schedules run smoothly, gave us bear hugs that could crush you in half, and cooked us meals that were soothing and delicious.

The next morning the classroom floor was slick, and Mrs. Knickerbocker was standing on one of our little chairs, hanging cupids and red hearts on the bulletin board that ran in a strip around the room. Her calves always looked bloated and her flowered dresses stopped just before the fullest part of her leg. She hopped down when she saw us enter and straightened her chunky necklace.

She seemed heated from hanging the Valentine decorations. "Be careful class, the floor is still wet from the mop!" Clearly, there were two sets of footprints—the high heels that Mrs. Knickerbocker was famous for and Vinny's. He wore rubber shoes with gigantic ridges on the bottom. The footprints were all mixed up and jumbled together in one corner of the solid green floor.

Alexander was already seated in his desk by the time I got to my own seat. Patty was watching me. I put my fingers up to my lips like I was smoking a cigarette to confirm that Alexander and I had smoked our first cigarette together last night in the garage. She wore a look of shock. I excused myself to go to the lavatory.

When I got to the lavatory the door was wide open, and Vinny's rusty bucket was being used as a doorstop. This meant that the bathroom was being cleaned and that you had to wait outside the door until Vinny was finished. I heard him whistling, "Oh my darlin', Oh my darlin', Oh my darlin',

Clementine, I have lost you, now I found you, Oh my dar-lin', Clementine!" Rather than going back to the classroom, I waited for Vinny to finish. He grabbed the bucket and let the lavatory door close itself. He stood there in the hallway with his equipment. All the classes were in session and the hallways were as quiet as I had ever heard them.

"Miss Olivia de Havilland."

Vinny had an odor—I was never sure if it came from the mop or his body.

"It's not Olivia de Havilland. It's Olivia Darnell. And I have to use the bathroom. Excuse ME."

The janitor lowered his already low voice and felt in his breast pocket just under the stitching that spelled "Vinny" in script. "Olivia—wanna cigarette?"

I couldn't move. I couldn't speak.

"What's the matter, Olivia? Don't tell me the cat's got YOUR tongue!"

I stared at him to see if he was kidding about the cigarette. He was already removing it from the pack. The crinkle of the hard cellophane was loud in the hallway. I grabbed it from his clammy hand and ran into the lavatory. I slipped on the wet floor and fell hard on my ass. I stashed the cigarette in my knee sock while still on the ground. I got up and pulled my skirt down so no one would see the long thin lump.

When I returned to class everyone was earnestly cutting red construction paper. I took my seat next to Alexander Lamb. Even though Alexander didn't say much, it was com-forting being next to him, elbow to elbow, working on our Valentine cards. He struggled trying to make his red paper heart perfect for me. I worked silently, nervous about the cigarette in my sock, and daydreamed about getting the finished Valentine from Alexander.

I brought Patty O'Mahoney home with me after school. My mother was home this time getting ready for her Valentine's Day party the following evening. She had Bernadette sweating from ironing linens and polishing silver. Surely, the party would not surprise my father who often said, "My wife is never home to greet me—unless she has fifty people home with her." Mrs. O'Mahoney was there, too, flitting from room to room, delighted to be hired by my mother to create flower arrangements. She hardly paid any attention to us, which was quite unusual. At the florist, she always had a carnation to pin to our uniform lapel, no matter the occasion.

I led Patty down to the garage and told her that since the Beatles were not practicing—my mother would never allow that kind of noise while she was preparing for her party—I would show her the spot where Alexander and I had smoked. The garage was quite large, big enough for three and a half cars, and Patty was frightened in the dark. Patty and Mrs. O'Mahoney both looked like double-processed blondes, and Patty was quite visible in the black space. "We're planning to do it again—here, I've got another stogie—that's what Alexander calls 'em." I removed the full-fledged cigarette from my knee sock, and Patty practically fainted.

Sometimes Patty talked about Alexander as though she knew him better than I did. She said, "It's so hard for me to picture Alexander smoking, you know, with that little chipmunk face and all."

I knew exactly what she meant. Alexander Lamb was good and tenderhearted. He had the qualities of a knight.

He struggled to get at the truth no matter how difficult. He worked hard at long division, his remainders would carry on to infinity, and he wouldn't even take the correct answers I offered him.

I was relieved when I heard Mrs. O'Mahoney call down to us, "What are you girls doing down there in the dark?"

When the eight-thirty bell rang on Valentine's Day every third grader was already sitting at their desks, hands folded, ready to say the Pledge of Allegiance and a prayer. I was feeling smug, because Alexander would hand me a beautiful Valentine that he'd made with his own gentle hands. And, I had brought the cigarette with me again in my sock, just in case he wanted to see it.

I looked over my shoulder for Patty. She was wearing a beautiful corsage made of the tiniest red roses I had ever seen. The miniature bunch was framed by a white lace doily in the shape of a heart and the tip of a silver arrow peaked out on one side of it. Patty looked warm and radiant. I felt pale in comparison to Patty; the red satin bow in my hair was pulled too tight and I could feel a headache starting in my temples.

Mrs. Knickerbocker was wearing her signature bright red lipstick but it seemed exceedingly vibrant on Valentine's Day. She had been fussing with herself all day and had on more bangle bracelets than usual, which really caused a distracting racket. Mrs. O'Mahoney said that if the school had enough teaching nuns, Mrs. Knickerbocker would probably have to find another career in another town. However, I knew that I could count on Mrs. Knickerbocker for leaving us sufficient time at the end of the school day so that we could exchange Valentine's Day cards before the three o'clock bell.

Our classroom door was wide open when we were told that it was time to exchange Valentines. Mrs. Knickerbocker stood right outside our classroom door to give us a little privacy. Every moment or two she would poke her head in the door to check our behavior, leaving part of her body in the hallway for Vinny to admire.

The kids in our third grade were giddy, darting all over the room, throwing cards at one another to bypass introductions. Some picked the candy hearts off the floor and read the imprints on them like "Be mine" before popping them in their mouths. Patty was standing alone by the window, being shy. I was making my way over to her to see why she was ignoring me when Alexander stepped in front of me with an armful of handmade things. My heart stopped. I had been waiting for him and his gentlemanly ways all day. I hadn't been able to find him at recess so I'd figured he'd been saving himself for our meeting now. He looked more handsome than usual in his gray trousers and navy blue jacket. He was wearing a red vest in the same exact shade as my hair ribbon. That, too, meant that fate had a plan for us.

Alexander Lamb said, "Excuse me, Olivia." The Valentine he labored over was in his hands in front of his heart. His little chipmunk face was pink.

"You're excused," I said to him in a flirtatious manner, and a sigh escaped me just the way my mother's did. I was so close I could see the water in Alexander's eyes. But he stepped in front of me and made it over to the window where Patty stood beaming in her blonde hair and red rose corsage. With a sweetness I have never seen before, he placed his Valentine in Patty's hands.

The three o'clock bell must have rung, because I was suddenly alone. In the back of the classroom, I stood holding my own Valentine creation for Alexander and noticed a small circle of dried vomit with granules and red candy hearts lying on top of it. It was a bit of a shock since I hadn't gotten a whiff of it once all day. Mrs. Knickerbocker grabbed her purse and told me to stop daydreaming and to get going. She had an important meeting and couldn't wait all day for me to get a notion to leave. Then she was gone.

I threw my Valentine in the overflowing garbage and stood facing the old chipped statue of Mary. A finger was missing on her left hand but the right hand was all there. I took the cigarette from my sock and stuck it in between her plaster fingers as if the holy woman was about to take a long drag off Vinny's cigarette.

# HOLY WATER

Mom stopped short to admire the potted Easter lilies lining the steps to the altar. She wore a pantsuit the color of a camel and carried a pony skin bag. I watched her face brighten and wondered if the tall lily reminded her of something—maybe her own figure? It was a pleasure she was keeping all to herself, because I didn't deserve the easy exchange of conversation. I was in punishment for an ordinary lie, "a forgery" she called it. Tests from school have to be signed by a parent, but I signed her name myself. Mom said this was just the icing on a trail of lies.

"You know what they say about us, Louise, don't you? 'Oh, how the mother dresses, how immaculate she is—not a wrinkle on her—and a widow at her age—imagine! But look at that little girl. A piggy. How did a piggy come from that woman?' That's just what they say, as sure as I'm standing here." She smoothed her hips with her palms, the way she did in front of her full-length mirror in the mornings, while studying my unkempt hair.

I followed her with my head down, counting the square tiles with swirls of buff marks, relieved to be as quiet as a mouse in my Keds as her heels echoed. I shot a quick glance at the main statue of Mary with those marble ball eyes; her presence was nothing compared to the aura that followed my mother.

We walked through the door to the left of the altar and

stepped into the Waiting Room. As if she were washing off something sticky, Mom swished her fingers around in the holy water held by the cupped hands of a stone angel embedded in the wall.

Monsignor Archer, the pastor, was so tall he had to dip down to come through the doorway. "Loretta, Loretta," was all the priest said to Mom, but those two words wafted above us like a soothing hymn. Monsignor and Mom faced each other, holding hands.

As president of the Ladies' Auxiliary of St. John of the Cross, Mom supervised luncheons and bazaars. She oversaw Carmine, the janitor who worked for the church, and she was in charge of the small storage rooms behind the altar where cleaning supplies were kept, the ones which made the church shine and smell of lemon oil.

Carmine walked in with a carton of votives under his arm and took us all by surprise, because he was dressed as an altar boy—black, ankle-length robe with white smocking—just out of reverence. He was only as tall as the cherubs, swarming in stone ribbons and piled one upon another at the entrance doors. His crew cut was the color of chalk and stood like the edge of our front lawn.

How often I have watched him from my seat in Mass, along with the rest of the fourth graders, and wondered if the interior life the priest was talking about at the pulpit was the same interior life that was going on in Carmine's head. He'd be fidgeting around at the base of the pulpit, unnoticed, with that rag hanging out of his back pocket in the midst of the consecration. A perfect misfit angel left behind.

"Keep Louise busy, Carmine. She's all yours," Mom said,

ignoring Carmine as she walked over to study the loopy script on the wall behind him. She must have been reminded of my forgery.

Monsignor Archer watched me and Carmine like we were midgets on a floor about to do a trick.

"I'll be down by St. Frances, kiddo," Carmine winked.

When he left, Mom reached for Monsignor's hands again.

I left them there to start my own jobs and walked down the skinny hall with dimly lit sconces that didn't light a path to anything. I practically felt my way around and found Dominga, the rectory's laundress, ironing a purple vestment in the Priests' Dressing Quarters. One wall was papered with Latin Prayers so the priest about to say mass could read them aloud while he put on his vestments. Everything in Latin sounded like *hamandeggshamandeggshamandeggs*. The open window was cut out of stone in the shape of a top hat. I loved the smell of fresh air and starch and wondered why it didn't improve Dominga's mood. She had a white towel under the ironing board to prevent the heavy starch from forming a sticky area on the wooden floor.

"Louise, get me the basket, please."

I found the laundry basket near the chest of small drawers that, normally, I would have investigated when Dominga was gone. Not anymore. I was afraid to pick up the basket because it overflowed with the altar napkins the priests used to wipe their lips, after drinking wine from the chalice. Red crosses, neatly stitched into each one, were probably sewn in by the blind.

Dominga hung the vestment on the door and punched tissue paper in the sleeves before starting on the pile. "Louise,

I suppose you want the cookies before you get started." She dished out this omen with her back facing me. Usually, her droopy eyes hung at half-mast, but apparently, they didn't miss anything.

The nuns baked sugar cookies with lard and left them around on plates with doilies. You couldn't even take one on the sly, because each cookie left a grease mark. It was just one more thing you had to get permission for.

"No, thank you. I'm going to help Carmine now."

"Don't forget. If you want one, you have to ask."

"I know, I know."

"I know you all right, Lady Jane."

This new honest life was easier than I had imagined, especially if you started the new life in the Priests' Dressing Quarters, behind the altar, with the hiss of Dominga's iron in your ear. It was sort of like the nuns' lives, doing chores, praying, teaching others by your own unassuming behavior. Mom said all that was easy-as-pie, if you didn't have children under your feet.

I was drawn to the tall, ornate silver chalice, the top of which had been removed and placed beside it on the mission table; the handle was an empty crucifix. We had a similar line-up of sterling silver at home on the buffet table in our dining room: candelabras, goblets, coffee and teapots with creamers of the same family. This chalice, however, had a majestic presence. If only humble St. Anthony had the same confident attitude, he might get more followers. The chalice stood alone with a certain kind of bravery, like an oversized toy soldier or a statue that could breathe and walk away.

The spell it cast forced me to walk right up to it for a

peek inside. I had had the same feeling once before when looking inside a birds' nest. Inside the silver chalice, I saw a small mound of hosts, as clean and white as the sponge of Angel's Food Cake. Each wafer appeared firm and soft like the napkins in Dominga's "finished pile."

I hadn't received my first Holy Communion yet. I had one year to go. When St. John's Grammar School attended Mass, the younger grades watched the older ones receive. Even the most rotten kids in the school could go up and get the wafer and look holy with heads bent, hands folded in front of their hearts.

It was so hard to wait for the taste. The flavor was a mystery I couldn't get out of my head, more compelling than the Trinity. Once I asked Mom to describe the flavor, and she said, "It's like nothing else I ever had."

During our first Friday Mass of the school year, I had watched the faces of the kids on the way back to their seats, with hosts in their mouths, their eyes practically closed for a fine performance. Chuckie Sutton, with the straight, straight hair that swung back and forth when he walked, was always scraping it from the roof of his mouth like a wad of gum. I bet my life that it was Chuckie who spat the host out on the floor and never owned up to it. I had stared at it, too, that day, on the dirty floor under the pew. It was consecrated, it had life in it. I had expected it to quiver with movement the way Mexican jumping beans did when they were left in the sun.

Carmine had found the host on the floor while he was cleaning, and the entire school was called into the gym over the PA system by Father Sweeney. Later, at recess, Chuckie told me he saw Carmine carrying the host like a hot potato, running, his hand swaddled in the chalice napkin.

During the reprimanding, the rosaries that hung from Father's belt made a clinking tempo, a light-hearted backbeat to his speech. The purple-blackish circles under his eyes proved he was the talking dead, and, he belched in the middle of his thoughts. "One of you—and God knows who you are—took the very body of Jesus Christ—our very nourishment," he bowed then, thumping his chest with his fist. "The privilege of being a Catholic, and cast it down to the dirty soles of your very own feet."

"God knows me, too, I guess," I said out loud, leaving the Priests' Dressing Quarters. *But, does He know what I'm thinking?*

I began to imagine myself as a Holy Helper with a lace veil, an image God would easily pick up while he scanned brains throughout the world. I was on the lookout for holy water, so I, too, could dip my finger in and make the sign-of-the-cross over my forehead and chest at one fell swoop the way Mom did. I managed to keep a tablespoon of it in the palm of my hand, in case I ran into cripples. This picture in my mind—a girl driven by good deeds—was overtaken by the image of the silver chalice.

It was dark in the church, but certainly lighter than the hallway where I had come from on a mission. The faint smell of incense hung in the church during the Easter season, a smell that reminded me of the Hare Krishnas in New York City.

I saw Carmine down by the statue of St. Frances, the

saint who was forever surrounded by birds and babies without diapers. Carmine stood there with one hand in his side pocket the way President Kennedy did on TV before he got shot, which gave him a relaxed look. He was talking in his hushed voice to Mrs. Fanning, another Auxiliary member, who stood with her retarded daughter, Maddy. They came every Saturday afternoon to help Mom prepare the church. It was too late to turn around and escape Maddy, who was twice my size and width.

Maddy was as strong as a man and clamped my head between her short arm and ribcage. She rubbed my face and head with the palms of her hands, the way the bowlers in the league shined their bowling balls on Friday nights. Her fingers smelled like Silly Putty.

Carmine freed me, reminding me again of how his janitor job was just a cover-up for his godly ways. "Madeline," he called in the loudest whisper possible without offending the near silence he lived in. Carmine took the long wooden stick used for lighting votives, held it in front of Maddy's eyes, and then tipped it back to his own eyes like a metronome, hypnotizing her. Maddy's eyes darted from Carmine, then down to my head (still rubbing and mashing), then back to Carmine. Maddy's eyes were never quite still. Her gaze was set on the open space in front of her, as if she were watching a little show, a theatrical performance just for her. Then she clapped her hands heartily, finally dropped me, and gave in to Carmine's power.

I looked, too, from the floor to see what he had in his eyes. More theatre, maybe, but whatever it was, the tornado in Maddy swirled to a halt.

At this point, while watching all this, Mrs. Fanning's shoulders fell. She was the only one in the whole place who reminded me of a saint. Mom referred to her as "Poor Deirdre Fanning with the Mongoloid." Carmine referred to the girl as "The Chosen One." Although I think Mrs. Fanning would have preferred to be in Mom's shoes, because she treated Mom with a reverence you could serve a queen with.

Mrs. Fanning, seeing her daughter settled and safe, "working" with Carmine, left us there to start her own duties. Any time away from Maddy must have been a relief for her, even if it meant polishing brass in St. John's.

"Take these from the carton underneath the grotto and put them in here," Carmine instructed us. He held the votive candles one by one like doves in the palms of his hands and then placed each one gently in the jars to demonstrate. My neck throbbed. Maddy rocked herself, staring into the flames. I was the only one following instructions.

"Good job," Carmine said to Maddy.

Carmine got up from his knees, although you could barely tell there was a difference between him kneeling and standing.

"Oh, come on, Carmine, please. You promised," I begged, afraid he would leave me alone with this girl. She'd get me under her arm again and mash a lit votive in my face, scarring me for life. Maybe this was part of Mom's punishment for me.

The church was cold, even in the month of May, and there were two sparrows flitting up near the basilica-style ceiling, the way they get caught in the supermarket sometimes.

Carmine stayed and now I was getting the fixed look from him. I continued to work, and he knelt down next to me. I felt pressure pass through my chest, slowly, the way they say a soul passes through you if you are next to a loved one when they die. Carmine put his hand on my shoulder. I felt too humble to look up at him. Closing my eyes, I let my mind go blank. I didn't let myself think back to the chalice, filled to the brim with hosts.

Carmine put his head down, his lips moving like those old ladies who sat in the back of the church praying madly with their fist of rosaries over their hearts. He did this, too, while he worked. He was doing it now.

He looked up, and, at first, I thought he spotted the birds. "I have to help Jesus," he said.

"With what?"

"Gotta help him carry the cross." He looked down the middle aisle with worry and dread, as if it were the steep hill of Calvary. I looked there and saw no one.

I was surprised by this. I realized Carmine, like me, played pretend games, but he was almost too good at it.

"Louise—you have work to do!" He swiped my nose jokingly and everything was back to normal.

He got up from his knees, made the sign of the cross, and headed down the aisle. I noticed he had changed his outfit to his usual three sweaters, all in different sizes.

The organist was practicing "Someone's Crying My Lord" and with all her stopping and starting it sounded like she was playing musical chairs. Maddy was humming her own tune, and I figured it was safe to leave her while she was in a trance.

On my way to the Priests' Dressing Quarters, I pretended to be a weeping lady of Jerusalem, although I wished I could have turned the lights up.

"Let me help you, dear Jesus." I took the edge of my cardigan sweater and patted the sweat off Jesus' brow but it got caught on the crown of thorns. I pulled it away, gently, and let Jesus continue up the hill of Calvary, carrying the huge cross that looked like two wooden beams ripped out of the church's ceiling.

"Don't worry," I said to Jesus. "Carmine will be back to help you lift that thing."

I took off my sweater and held it up to catch a little bit of light to see if Jesus left the imprint of his face on my sweater, but there was nothing.

Dominga was gone. The ironing board was pushed over to the side, and the cord was wrapped neatly around the iron. The purple vestment that hung from the top ledge of the door, stuffed with paper, nearly gave me a heart attack. The undergarments, the white gown and sash, were all laid out on a serving board so the priest could dress easily while praying.

"Dominga," I whispered, to be sure. Clearly, she had left for the bus.

A breeze from the open window skimmed my face. Outside, there was green beading on the trees. I was alone with the chalice that held the hosts that weren't even blessed.

I figured I better check to see if anyone was around. I walked out of the Priests' Dressing Quarters and came face to face with a brilliant Lucifer embedded in stained glass, his bushy eyebrows and scowl were identical to Mother Thomas Aquinas's, our school principal.. His muscular arm was ready to reach out of the window and scoop you from the hallway if you looked his way.

I kept going. The doors to all the rooms were closed

except one. It was open, just a crack. The sign on the door said Storage. That's where Carmine kept the spare kneeling benches, tall screens for the confessional boxes, and cartons of candles and lighting sticks. I often played in there when Mom worked; the stacked cartons made great hiding places.

I heard whispers. I looked through the opening to the Storage Room and saw Mom. The cloud of shame came over me, but then it rose and drifted over to her. She looked like she was having a special private confession, without the screen between her and her priest. In fact, I don't think a screen would have fit between them. Monsignor Archer was standing straight and tall, his head tilted back toward heaven. Mom was kneeling down in front of him so that her head came to where his belly button would be, if he had one over his robe. The one beam of light in the whole place exposed a simple smile on her face, as if she were on stage. Their hands were in an unusual hold—palm to palm, fingers straight—sharing their interior lives as if they were the only two people in the world. They talked so low and lovingly, I wished I could hear their words.

I could see it was true what Mom said. There was a peacefulness about this Monsignor. Everything seemed to slow down around him. I watched Monsignor Archer gently bring Mom to her feet, and he put her hands over his face. He breathed so hard, his nose between her fingers; I heard him loud and clear.

While their interior lives were mingling, I left and went straight into the Priests' Dressing Quarters. I could picture Dominga, waiting for the bus with that usual smirk on her face. Now the wooden floors creaked and moaned like an invisible alarm system. I picked up the pile of napkins and started walking in circles around the room in a path that would indicate to anyone entering that I was just doing my job, placing the ironed napkins in the "finished" basket.

The circles I made drove me to the chalice each time. The hosts began to look like hors d'oeuvres. After all, Carmine said, "A host is no different than toast, until the priest changes it into the body of Christ."

I wondered if Monsignor Archer could change Mom's body and blood into something else, too. He changed the expression on her face so it looked as if it belonged to a different woman.

I circled by the chalice and then reached over like a batter taking a practice swing. Just then I heard the cheerful voices of Mom and Monsignor coming down the hallway. The church bazaar was coming, and Mom was delegating again, telling the priest that she was making changes after last year's fiasco (before she was President). The door swung open, and, for the first time all day, Mom stood there looking pleased with me.

"I was just straightening up, Mom. Hello, Monsignor. Were you doing the silver—want me to finish for you? Look, I have the rags right here." I pulled one out of the bag and shook it.

I expected Mom to walk over to the chalice and slam the top back on, because she always said she had a hunch about me.

"No. We had our meeting down in the Waiting Room with Mrs. Fanning and some of the other ladies on the committee. Our Spring Bazaar is right around the corner."

I looked at Mom, right in the eyes, the way she did to me when she had me cornered, but she was looking up at the priest. I waited for the cloud of shame to drift in after her. As I stood there, I remembered Dad describing her as a tall glass of water, and, for the first time, I could see what he meant. She really was an imposing sight, standing there with Monsignor Archer. They looked like beautiful giants, their cheeks flushed pink, their brushed-back hair sandy and wavy like brother and sister. Mom said Monsignor was the most handsome father she had ever seen, but I never saw him that way. He was a priest with a brimless hat, and Chuckie Sutton said he kept two mice under it.

Monsignor had a distracted, concerned look on his face, which spread over to Mom's. "Smoke?" They both said it at the same time, the way my grandparents say the same things at the same time, because they've been married so long.

"Stay here, Louise—we'll be right back."

I could smell it, too, and my eyes began to sting. But I continued my chores. I circled by the chalice, picked up a host, and placed it in my mouth, without ever stopping in my tracks.

"Amen," I said promptly and dropped the basket. With my head down and my hands folded in prayer over my heart, I pressed my tongue on the host and braced myself.

Whoever baked them left out the sugar. Even the cookies with the lard had a little taste. Now I knew why Chuckie was always scraping the roof of his mouth—it got so dry I had to use my fingernail to get it out of my teeth. Who could blame him for spitting it out?

Mom appeared, alone now, pulling me by the elbow. "Thank God we're right by the exit."

"Fire. A real fire? Mom, I have to find Carmine. And, Maddy. I gotta get her, too."

In my mind, all I could see was Maddy, sitting by the candles, rocking.

I tore from Mom, but she grabbed the straps of my overalls through my cardigan. The crotch of my pants jerked and tightened. "Mom, what about Carmine? What if—"

"What if, what if. Oh, Louise, don't you get it? Don't you ever get it? You're old enough now. He's not right. Carmine's not right in the head."

I couldn't move. All I saw was Carmine's watery eyes when he left me filling the jars.

"We have to help him."

Mom pushed me through the heavy door under the exit sign and shoved me hard into the cool, fresh air. It smelled like burning leaves, but it was spring.

We stopped near the birdbath by the path to the rectory. It was filled with fake grass and plastic Easter eggs. There was another statue of Mary there, too, and this one had a powder blue cape made of rain slicker material tied around her concrete neck. The wind kicked up, raising her cape up and down in the air, as she looked solemnly over at the eggs.

Thanks to the blaring fire alarm, the few of us who were in the church must have made it out safely. Carmine and Maddy, too, if not from the back door, then one of the others that were studded all around the sides of St. John's.

Mom steered me further away to the parking lot, where I saw the tail of Mom's turquoise El Dorado sticking out of her usual spot. We were lucky. There were no flames, just a little smoke. Now, in the relief of safety, it was the perfect time for her to tell me all the things moms tell their daughters.

"Louise." Mom whispered, looking around to be sure we were alone.

"Yes?"

"I want you to get me a couple of Easter Lilies from the altar and put them in the trunk of the car. The church has too many anyway."

I was unable to answer, but she wasn't waiting for my response as she brushed suddenly visible lint from her jacket. Mom looked different out here in the sun. There was something tough about her, a streak that didn't mesh with her looks. You really had to know her like I did to know you couldn't cross her. The lipstick she had applied so carefully was smudged and faded to a brownish color.

I studied her more closely and looked for the lie she'd just told me about where she'd been and what she had been doing. That particular lie didn't seem ordinary at all. I remembered the long double-thick shadow on the wall in the storage room formed by her and her priest.

Now her arms were folded across her chest, and I could tell she was dying for a cigarette. She took the pony skin bag from her shoulder, opened it, and pulled out a plastic bottle of Lourdes water, the one that comes from the Grotto found by Bernadette. Mom quickly opened the bottle, and I was sure she was going to take a quick swig, but all she did was dab a little behind her ear, put the cap back on, and throw it back in her bag. Then I noticed the cardboardy taste in my mouth. It was a piece of God, or would-be God, right there next to a cavity with a silver filling. For a moment I wished

I had never stolen the host so I would have something to look forward to. The speck disintegrated in my mouth as we waited for the tall figure of Monsignor Archer, in his long, inflated robes, to come around the church building.

# PAST THE CLUBHOUSE

The four of us stood under a magnolia on the corner, near Larchmont Shore Club, by Lynn and Jay's house. Lynn and Jay Wyeth were brother and sister. I was going to be with Jay, and Lynn was going to be with Jay's friend Fletcher Dunne. Fletcher stood with us, too, his bottom lip hanging just enough so you could see the jail on his teeth, but all I thought of when I looked at him, every time I looked at him, was his blind father and dead mother.

Jay, with all his smarts and calculations, was figuring out how we could get into Fletcher's father's basement without *interference*. This was one of his words. Jay stood there with his collar turned up under his bomber jacket, which later would teach me the smell of a boy. He went over the plan again and again until we got it straight, using his hands as if he was a man at a podium. He never once looked me in the eye while talking *strategy*.

Fletcher stared with a blank expression out into the street at nothing while Jay strategized. I figured this look was passed down to him from his father.

I'd heard that Mr. Dunne had a decent job that allowed him to work from home, probably with Braille and tape recorders. Jay said this fact had never been *verified*.

Fletcher never uttered a word to anyone about his blind dad or his dead mother, not even to Jay, so we all had to rely on rumors, especially as to how his dad had become blind in the first place. Jay told Lynn and Lynn told me that the events leading up to the fatal accident, which killed Fletcher's mother and caused his father's blindness, were *horrific*.

The powerful whacks of tennis balls from the club's courts were so loud I felt them in my chest, and I couldn't help but look in that direction, where the green canoes were piled high up against the fence, stacked like empty clam shells. But Jay was so focused on our plan the noise never disturbed his concentration. "What's the big deal?" I said. Everyone looked at me, and I immediately realized that I could not explain what I meant in front of Fletcher.

Jay checked his watch, following his own advice to *synchronize*.

"Never mind," I said.

It was so much easier to kiss Jay than to talk to him. I'm not sure we ever talked, except while kissing, about the kissing. He was teaching me, and he said it might take us several Saturdays to *perfect* it.

Everyone started to walk toward Fletcher's house, but I hung back. Of course, Jay noticed, but I was still surprised that he slowed and walked next to me.

I kept my gaze forward and said, "All we have to do is sneak in the Dunne's basement. Mr. Dunne might be able to pick up the vibrations in the floor, but he will never see us. We're lucky he doesn't have a dog. The seeing eye kind."

"He will never be able to *verify our identities*."

This was our first real exchange.

Jay yelled up to his sister. "Elizabeth made a good point." He ran ahead to catch up to Lynn, who was kicking dead leaves aside with her feet, making a path. It looked like getting into a basement to make out was the last thing on her mind.

We walked through the well-worn trail of Palmer Woods, and I was the last in line. I followed Lynn's skinny legs. She hopped on stones, jumped across the littered stream, and motioned to me to hurry. Her agility reminded me of the way she did math, scratching her way down the sheet of problems without hesitation.

"Lynn. Lynn!" I had to say her name several times to get her attention. "Fletcher's Dad will never see us."

"Oh *really*."

"What I mean is—why is Jay making such a production out of it?"

"He makes a production out of everything. Besides, if that doesn't work, why don't we just go to your house? No one's there either."

When we came out of the woods we were in New Rochelle, and Fletcher took the lead. As we approached the Dunne house, everything about it said 'blind man lives here.' The shades were drawn and the bushes were all straggly, not like the ones at the Wyeth house, which were carved into clubs and diamonds. Three cats by the door acted hungry.

We followed Fletcher up the driveway, past a Weber grill, and into the garage, where he made an effort to walk around the huge black stain on the floor. Jay poked his sister and pointed. The look on his face was talking evidence, as if this stain had something to do with everything. Seconds later, we were in the basement, spinning ourselves in chairs shaped like barrels.

Fletcher got up and went into the bar area to hunt for sodas. I went with him, because I always felt like the odd-man-out whenever I was alone with Lynn and Jay. They had their own language and never shared the definitions—like the word *ginge*. *What's the ginge?* they would say to each other, right in front of me. I know they made it up as some kind of signal.

"So," I said, watching Fletch, surprised that he wasn't concerned with the racket he was making, "at least we can use your house, I mean, seems like no one is home."

"Like your house," he said in his usual blandness.

I wanted to say that I didn't have a blind man hiding upstairs, but I didn't have the heart.

"You don't have to pretend with me," Fletch said, standing on an upside-down Dewar's crate, looking up on a top shelf. The seat of his jeans appeared empty. I know all about your mother." I was such a jerk. I had been so afraid to upset him, and there he was, handing me a soda like he already forgot he was out of line. He should have known something about what it felt like. My mom hadn't been in a horrific accident, she'd just floated away.

"Here," he said, "carry these."

"Thanks a lot."

He gave me the once over like he was checking me out, but I knew this couldn't be. Everyone liked Lynn better.

I walked to the other side of the basement and held the can of soda over Lynn's head, waiting for her to take it. She had fallen off the barrel laughing, and I wondered how anyone could kiss a boy with her brother in the room. She grabbed the bottle of Coke and immediately chugged it.

For the first time all day, Jay stared at me. I feared my embarrassment accentuated the apples of my cheeks, which were bigger than anyone else's, and for which I was always self-conscious. I had let my hair grown long to hide them, and it seemed that I was growing into the name Jay teased me with, when we were alone.

"Hey, Pocahontas," he said, crawling to me on his hands and knees.

I could not believe that Lynn and Fletcher were already going at it on the couch, their heads bobbing. Jay and I always had to work up to it.

Jay put his head on my lap and looked up at me, but I couldn't look down, not with those slurping sounds. He didn't seem to hear it, his intensity shifted in my direction. I focused on the framed print over the fireplace of kittens crawling out of a basket.

My hair hung in my face, and Jay took a lock and studied it. At first I thought he was looking for split ends, but he began to use it like a soft paintbrush, brushing his lips and then his eyes, which were closed.

He sat up and held my face, his two strong thumbs pressing into my heated cheeks, and kissed me. My nose pressed so hard against him that I had to maneuver my head so I could breathe. He stopped and looked at me. Then he put his hand on my chest, and began to outline, with his finger, the form he felt underneath my shirt. All I could think of was the blue and pink flowered bra I was wearing, the one I'd bought at Wanamaker's, while my father sat outside in his car and smoked a cigar.

I felt a warm gush in my underwear. Great. I had white jeans on.

"What's the matter, Poke?" He smiled, looking at me carefully, taking his hands away, assuming he had done the wrong thing.

I noticed our hair was exactly the same brown-black, but his eyes were light blue.

"I really have to go to the bathroom."

"Hey—Fletch," he said, twisting his neck but keeping his body in the same place. "Elizabeth has to go. Fletch. Fletch. Oh, Fletch," he said, dragging out the "oh."

"Gotta go upstairs," he responded as Lynn pulled him right back down.

"What about Mr. Dunne?" I whispered in Jay's ear, my lips mistakenly touching his soft lobe.

Now he was talking into my ear, his lips very deliberately on my lobe. "Sounds like no one is up there. And, look at Fletch here. Does he seem worried? Besides, we would have heard *discriminatory* sounds by now."

"Well, you don't hear too much when you don't want to."

"Only when I'm *fixated*." He pulled me to him and we were back in his warm mouth.

When I got up, the taste of him was familiar, like I had known it my whole life. And, I felt something genuine from him for the first time. He was looking at me, directly in the eye.

"Do you want me to go with you?"

"No, it's OK."

"I am *lying-in-wait* then."

I began up the stairway. It turned a corner and led to the next floor. I tiptoed up the steps and opened the door slowly. I could see part of the living room, with furniture positioned around the perimeters, as if the middle was left for dancing. I heard the hum of the refrigerator and the ice cubes dropping from the icemaker into the freezer bin.

The room next to the kitchen, where a bathroom might be located had a closed door. I crept down the hallway, thinking I really did look like Pocahontas with my hushpuppy slip-ons and my shirt with the fringe. Now the creeping.

I used the bathroom and washed my hands with cold water. There was no soap in the soap dish, and the towel was damp. My face looked flushed in the mirror. When I came out, I didn't bother creeping.

"You're not Fletch."

I stopped. I saw the figure of Mr. Dunne sitting at a desk in front of the window in the living room. I was sure he had not been there before.

"No, Mr. Dunne."

"Ah, one of Fletch's girlfriends."

"I'm just a friend," I said, wanting to make that clear and feeling lucky he couldn't see the disgust in my face. "I'm sorry. I had to use the bathroom."

"Don't be sorry. If you have to go, you have to go."

Mr. Dunne, seated at the empty desk, stared out the picture window. He was lanky like Fletch, unshaven, in a wrinkled dress shirt, the cuffs flopped open. I wanted to ask him about all the things a blind man can't do; I could count a few just by looking at him.

"And, you are…?"

"Elizabeth. Elizabeth Pearly. Lynn Wyeth's friend," I quickly added, since that is how I was referred to. The Wyeths had me practically living at their house, thinking they were helping my father.

"Yes, I knew your parents from the Shore Club."

A cat appeared at my feet, surprising me. I petted it, and its scratchy meow frightened me.

"That's Tiger. He was one of the kittens."

He was talking like they were famous or something.

"What kittens?"

"One of the survivors."

He must have been talking about the horrific accident. God, I didn't want to know. I started to back up. Maybe he was referring to something else. How could a kitten be involved?

"You haven't heard this? Fletch hasn't told you?"

"No."

"Knowing Fletch, he was trying to spare you. He knows you have had your own troubles."

"Yes, he's kind that way," I answered, pleased he couldn't see me rolling my eyes. I sat down in the spot where I was standing because my legs were getting rubbery.

"There were three new litters and the basement area near the garage stunk," he began. "My wife couldn't stand it, said our house smelled like a shanty with all the cats and litter boxes."

I looked around to see if I could sneak away.

"There must have been eighteen. I had a solution in a tin can. No label on it. I doused the cement floors, thinking it would clean and disinfect. My wife came in, finishing a cigarette. She had a habit of tossing and stamping. Then, the explosion. She was my last vision. Now she is my only vision. Smoking a Winston," he added the last part like it was the best part.

"Oh." I said, feeling something similar. All this time, since Mom had died, the things I saw in my head—I never thought they were outside of me, they were just a part of me. "I see things, too."

It was as if he was staring at my forehead.

"What do you see?" he asked, his voice lower than before.

"I mean, I'm not sure. Sometimes I see my mother dragging the canoe on the beach. The green one. Then she's hopping in, floating out past the Clubhouse. It's foggy, then I lose track of her."

He turned back to face the window and rubbed his chin. Maybe he forgot I was there.

I managed to get up, trying not to make a sound, realizing his remaining senses must be more acute now.

"Come to the window here," he said.

I felt as if he was pulling on a rope tied around my waist. The room smelled like fireplace ashes. The window looked out onto the street, and it was getting dark.

"Look," he said. "You can come anytime and see your mom."

He must have been off his rocker, and Jay would love to know this tidbit. Now I was the only one who knew the whole story, the real story. I wasn't even sure of my own.

I could see his face, and he didn't look sad or blind. Just kind of mesmerized.

"What is your wife doing now?"

"Still smoking," he said. "In her way."

Maybe he was nuts, but I couldn't help myself. I walked to the window. Beyond the street, above the houses in front, I could see Mom in her canoe, her dark hair in a long unraveling twist down her back, paddling on one side in the air, then the other. "Mom," I called and waited. She didn't hear me.

I walked downstairs with the image of my mother with me. I moved in a trance, worried that I was like Mr. Dunne. We lived in our own kind of foursome. But I got to see my mom and that was all that mattered. I loved seeing her long delicate arms again, arms she used to put around me. I would keep that for myself.

When I entered the basement, Lynn said, "We stopped sucking face because you took so long. We were about to come up and get you. Look at her Jay, she looks *mal*."

Even Fletch didn't know what that meant in the Wyeth language. I wondered if he knew what his father was up to up there. Hardly a decent job with Braille.

Fletch looked up at me for quite a while, and we found ourselves in a stare contest. Jay was *riveted*.

I waited for a remark from Fletch, like 'Is *your* father any good at conjuring up *your* mother?' He stood up on top of a footstool, and made his announcement. "Yeah, she's *mal* alright. Whatever the fuck that means, she's it."

Lynn jumped up and gave him an exaggerated karate chop in the back of his neck, and when he fell back on the floor laughing, I noticed his lips were red and raw. I was sure I could see his tonsils dangling like punching bags.

Jay got up and put his arm around me, maneuvering me over to the bar area where we could be alone. He put me up on the high stool and sat on the one opposite, so our knees could interlock. All I wanted to do was go back upstairs. It was better to be with the crazy and the dead.

"Do you know what happened to my mother?" I asked him.

The detective look returned to his expression, as if he was coming upon the ultimate evidence that would close his case.

"Do you?" I repeated, feeling my throat close, knowing that I would never be able to ask again.

"Well," he said, stamping his lips on mine as if he was transferring a discovery that he had kept hidden all along. He pulled away and looked down at the floor. "I heard she did like the Indians do."

I pictured Mom in the canoe, placing her paddle inside, next to her feet. I pictured her rocking from side to side, going faster and faster until the flimsy canoe tipped over.

"You mean." I was never able to say the word that was worse than death, more than death.

"Yes," he said.

I watched him pick up my hand, but I didn't feel his touch. He had more to say, he always did.

"But, I'm not *gullible* like everyone else in this town," he said, finally looking up at me. "I'm sure it's only *hearsay*."

# EFFECTS OF THE WATERFRONT

After Dad died, I never dreamed I'd be able to get him back. As I dragged the skimmer over the pond, all I saw in my mind were the bulky hospital orderlies, joking with each other over Dad's body as they removed him from the bed. I studied this image, their heave-ho motions, my father's grand figure without him in it.

I flung the dead leaves off the net over my shoulder, paying no attention to the Koi that were hiding under the duckweed. I kept thinking about those orderlies—did they just grab his arms and feet and yank him off the bed? *One, two, three, upsy daisy old man,* or did they slide their forearms under his back and kind of roll him on the gurney before wheeling him down to the morgue? Did they stop at the soda machine for a Pepsi, leaving him under the sheets on the side of the hallway, waiting, while they checked out the uniformed asses on the thirteenth floor?

Ray and I had just moved into an old colonial on Mohegan Road. The house had a long driveway draped by weeping willow trees, a rose garden off to the right, and a fishpond in the shape of a bottom-heavy figure eight. The pond was surrounded by tufts of reeds that hunched over in the slightest breeze. In the back of our house, a silky body of water reflected purple clouds, a pattern that drifted into one swollen form after another with the sluggishness of cake batter.

The surrounding homes were too close for the privacy I had hoped for. Next door, the kids and their dog usually hung out in a small mass at the end of the driveway. If I stopped and listened, I could hear the rhythm of their voices, like the background noise of the Connecticut turnpike that was often punctuated by rumbles and blasts. Their faces always looked suspicious when I drove by them, and I figured that one day they would make their way over the fence and into our back-yard, a slow moving, single file line of vengeful Indians.

I should have left Dad's spirit in peace next to my moth-er at Memorial Fields cemetery. Instead, I decided to drive out to Cross Road Lane and Passage Way, the corner where their graves were located. This barren area of fresh plots had no shade, so, as a weeping mourner, you felt as though you were basting in your own juices. The only people I ever saw around were the gravediggers eating long sandwiches out of white paper, chewing and staring like blank-faced cows in a field.

I was in that depression again, and the only way I can describe it is to say that it was a deserted place. I told myself I could see Dad in my own way, whenever I felt like it, as clearly as I could see myself in the mirror. I got into my Jeep and sped down the long driveway to get Dad out of the grave, to stop this charade. I thought about his tactics, how he'd tried to soften my heart, which he'd described as an icy one. "You're not like your mother," he used to say. "She cried for everyone."

I drove, my head in a fog, to Memorial Fields. I was think-ing that this dying thing Dad had pulled on me was just like him. He always tried to rile me in one way or another. He used to try to get me going by telling me about his diabetic Mom. She died when he was a seven-year-old boy. Or, his sister, Edie, who died of an aneurysm when she was just eighteen and beautiful; he saw blood trickle out from the side of her mouth. The way he told me about her death, I could envision a hospital room in the hue of old linen, heating pipes hissing, one folding chair next to the bed, dragged in from the lounge, and a brick wall the shade of brown gravy and so close you could lean out the window and touch it. The only color in the room I could imagine was the blood on Edie's ivory skin. He told me his memories in all their versions. He had a knack for slipping in one heart wrenching detail. At that time, they didn't have the impact that they were having on me now.

I was lingering in the beginning stage of grief a little too long, unable to do much besides cook for Ray and clean out the fishpond. I wasn't moving on to the next step, the one after denial. But now that I had reached the mature age of thirty, who was to tell me that I couldn't have Dad back, that is, in my own way?

I arrived at the cemetery where Dad was buried. I got out of the Jeep and saw the family plot in the new section. The new part of the cemetery was terraced; the freshest plots on the highest level were mounded with heaps of cut flowers.

I walked to the grave and stared at Dad's chiseled name— Phillip Joyce, 1930-1996. I stood still, with my eyes closed, for a long time. I stood there so long I began to smell him— that mixture of heavy starch and Old Spice cologne, the same scent on his white dress shirt that I still kept hidden in the back of my closet. The warm breeze and thick air at the cemetery made his smell so intense it was almost too much. Now I could smell his neck. I opened my eyes, stared at the ground, and then closed them again. I felt my father; I felt the insides of his wide, thick-skinned palms, my hand in his. He came to life in me.

Dad was sitting on the edge of his gravestone, his cane hooked on his forearm as he relit his pipe, puffing steadily to get something going, and, after a few moments, I smelled the cherry tobacco. God, how I had missed that smell!

"You're late," he said. He lightly slid his dapper self from his seat, his sleeves rolled up to his elbows. His flushed cheeks made him appear ruddier than usual; the heat had already gotten to him.

"It took you this long to come and drag my ass out of here?"

"Look, Phil, it took me a while to figure it all out. I guess I'm not too bright."

Like so many times before, we felt suddenly parched.

"I could go for a cold one." He was writing something, stick-in-sand fashion with his cane, in the small bed of dirt at the bottom of the headstone.

When he got in the car I was taken aback by the unfamiliar musty smell of his clothes. He was usually so particular— hard creases down the legs of his pants, coordinated argyle socks. He always carried a small comb in his back pocket.

"Leaving Mom a note?"

He didn't answer me. I knew he was observing the way families decorated their plots with greenery or geraniums, and how some were lax.

First thing I did was drive Dad to our home. We got out of the Jeep, walked around back passed the semi-circle of rose bushes, and up the back steps, which took us through the screened porch and out to the back patio facing a small marina.

We sat on the wicker rockers, nursing a couple of bitter Heinekens. The cherry tobacco smoke stretched between us like floating taffy.

The boat basin across the way is an historical landmark, because of the old mill on the water's edge that used to grind grain in the early 1900s. The soldiers from the English army, during the revolution, camped out by the mill, directly across from our bedroom window, prior to their attack on nearby Greenwich, Connecticut. During the summer, after dusk, you can hear fireworks being shot from the amusement park half a mile away and see the sky flickering like a florescent light losing its juice. At times, the explosions tricked me into the sound and drama of a war being fought a stone's throw from our porch, the vibrations of the cannons and cherry bombs throbbing unevenly in my chest.

How often I would say to Ray, "Phil should see this place." There was nothing else my father liked better than to drink an ice-cold beer and feel the effects of the waterfront.

I had my chance now. "The Mohegans..." I paused to let him get the full sweep, his green eyes looking blue. "Kayaked from here and on out through those two islands." With the sun on the barn-red mill in the background, we watched the play of local history in front of us. I dreaded the thought of nighttime, when all this would turn pitch black and the mosquitoes would rise.

Dad raised his cane, poking the air in front of him, counting the slips across the way. He was an entrepreneur himself. There was a plate of old cheddar bits on water crackers on the wrought-iron table next to him, but he seemed only to be thirsty.

"You're really guzzling, Phil. No bars up there?" I was priming him; the whole shebang about what goes on after you die would come up out of him like a belch.

"Hey. I gotta get back. Your mother's gonna know something is rotten in Denmark."

"Shit, Phil. The least you can tell me is the availability of a cold one. Or, do you come from a hot place?"

Dad left the porch, drifted through the French doors, and into the house. They were stuck from the dense heat, but I yanked them open and trailed him. He was walking, more like gliding, away from me, on the hardwood floors, slowing to admire the early American crystal displayed in the china cabinets. He had a taste for elegant things. My living room curtains were full and deep. The raw yellow silk was draped away from either sides of the windows on brass rosettes before falling into long, fluted tails. I expected more of a reaction from him as his figure shimmied past them.

After his little tour, or whatever it was he was trying to prove, he went out the same way he came in—he was superstitious that way—and made his way to the car.

I followed him out to the Jeep. He was already sitting in the passenger seat when I unlocked my door. He was eyeing the Lynch kids down at the end of the driveway. I knew what he was thinking, but he didn't start in on me about having my own brats. I started the car and let the AC kick in full-blast. Dad was fiddling with the radio, looking for a Schubert

Waltz. He passed through every AM and FM station until he found what he wanted. It's funny how you forget the annoying habits of someone after they're gone.

"Phil, you never change. And, put on your seat belt. Shit. What's the difference now?"

Finally, Dad found a composition by Schumann: "Of Foreign Lands and Foreign People." I had played this song on the piano as a child, in simple form, while he'd sat in our backyard smoking his pipe. Now the song made his head drop back on the headrest as if he were slipping into a nice, hot bath.

"Haven't heard the good stuff in a while. Have you?"

My father's eyes closed again, the way they did on that first sip of beer.

"Jesus Christ!" I screamed to jolt him. "His mother!"

No reaction. *Fuck*, I thought, *at least call me a heathen for old time's sake.*

"So, Phil, do the tongues of fire pant over their heads—you know, the big dipper and the other two—the Father, the Son and the Holy Ghost? Do they sit on thrones, like those chairs we used to have in the basement? No one wears shoes, I know that—bet they have the native feet like me."

I turned off the radio.

Phil started to whistle a lusty melody. It sounded like an old German beer garden dance. His whistle was so powerful it always made me a little envious. The tune, performed with too much rubato, filled the car with his growing evasiveness. I probably wouldn't even miss him when he went back.

On the ride back to the cemetery, with Phil in the passenger seat like an outpatient, I knew I could snap him out of that trance by flooring the gas pedal. Frankly, I'd thought by now he'd be talking about all his relatives, his mom, his sister. I dreaded hearing about Edie. On the other hand, if he had seen her, I was more than willing to listen.

Dad pressed his own foot on the floor in front of him as if he had his own brake. We slowed down.

"You still have the lead foot—want to get yourself killed?"

"Is it worth it, Phil?"

He looked like he was thinking about other things.

"OK, good ole Phil has to get back before they lock the pearly gates. No time for his only daughter."

He fooled with the radio.

*So, this is what I get for suffering?* I was going to remind myself next time it wasn't worth it. Ever since Phil had died, there'd been a steady backbeat in my head. *Can you see me? Give me a sign? Having too good a time?* And, just as often, it went like this: *Don't look now.*

When we arrived at the grave I had an overwhelming urge to see Mom. Soft-shell crabs were in season now and the three of us could go out to The White Wharf on the harbor like we used to and order those frosted daiquiris. Just to see Mom, dressed to kill, wearing a lobster bib, would make me feel better.

Phil rose out of the car and looked a lot worse than when I had picked him up. I watched him drift over to the family plot. He positioned himself on top of his grave, holding his cane in midair like King Neptune. He sparkled in the blinding sun, hovering over the two coffins that lay beneath.

I put the car in reverse and parked. I got out, running zigzag over the sod, over all the bodies lying side by side in a six-feet-under ward, the cool dirt like filling spread between them. I became aware of my feet, stepping on the graves, knocking on the doors of the dead, causing enough of a reverberation to nudge them awake.

Dad used to warn me: Never walk on top of the souls six feet under, it makes them restless.

When I got to the grave, he was gone. I began the same routine. I stared hard. I closed my eyes. I opened my eyes. The smell of him came to me, but it was the musty one.

"Phil! Where the hell are you? Can't take the heat?" I laughed at his predicament. "No beers where you're going."

I looked out over the horizon of headstones. He had been so colorful in his clothes; he even wore pink sometimes. If he were there, he would stand out against the green like a gangly flamingo.

The woman tending a grave in the next row watched me. She started to come toward me, a Hitchcock-type housewife, now a widow, dressed in a shift with a small trowel in her hand.

*Go back to your support group.* I ignored her and headed back to my car. I remembered the day of Dad's funeral, the sound of the dirt dropping on top of his coffin. I could hear the sound now. It was caught in my ears. I had been so angry at the dirt that day. It had been dark, rich soil, the kind that was good for planting tomatoes. I'd hated myself for not fighting for him, for not getting him out of there. I had barely enough energy to kiss the red rose in my hand and throw it on top of him. I stood there long after others had left, picturing him inside his fancy coffin, his feet upright and stiff, like they had never been in life, with that dour look on his face.

I got back in the Jeep and checked the side and rear view

mirrors for Dad to pop up again. He'd do something like that to throw me a curve. Driving through the maze of the old section, I noticed a mausoleum in the shape of a loaf of bread, covered with English ivy, a bunch of fresh white flowers tied to the handle of the iron door. I drove out the narrow exit, guilty, thinking I'd better start planting petunias.

At home, I walked out to the porch where Dad and I had been just a little while earlier. The untouched dish of cheese and crackers was still there on the end table. I sat in the rocker and finished the beers as boats pulled up to the dock after a calm day, their passengers tossing anchor lines.

I looked out, between the islands, and saw two Mohegans kayaking toward me, hootin' and hollerin', their tomahawks raised above their heads. I sat up, startled back into reality, and when they moved closer, I saw it was the Lynch children, sunburned, with snorkels banded to their temples, floating haphazardly on their paddle boat. I helped myself to a cracker, which had lost its freshness in the salty humidity, and watched the old mill turn as it had so many years ago.

# Acknowledgements

A deep-hearted thank you to my husband, Mark Rossi, an impatient person who has shown my eccentric writing habits great patience. To my son, Ryan, a startling creative who inspires me with his unique vision and work ethic. Un grand merci to my daughter, Caitlan, my writing comrade and in-house editor. I would also like to thank my brother, poet Kevin Pilkington, who has shared this 'writing bit' with me our entire lives and never fails to support me. And, to his wife, Celia, my trusted reader and dear friend.

Thank you, Bob Fogarty, longtime editor of *The Antioch Review,* for making me remind my writer-self of a few things. For their consistent support: Tom Pilkington, Carlene Edwards, Ernesto Quinonez, Ray Bradbury, Peter Orner, Kevin McIlvoy, Mary Morris, Sheila Kohler, Suzanne Rossowski, Regina Ross, Jim Rosenwald, and Nancy Swallow. And to all my friends who read these stories along the way.

Infinite thanks to the charming Jaynie Royal, editor-in-chief and founder of Regal House Publishing, a visionary who believed in my fiction, and just gets it every time.

I feel so indebted to my meticulous and kind editor, Pam Van Dyk. And, to the entire Regal Team, thank you.

And, finally, in remembrance of my parents, Jack and Lillian Pilkington, the most generous of all characters.